Taboo

Voices of Women in Uganda on Female Genital Mutilation

Taboo

Voices of Women in Uganda on
Female Genital Mutilation

Edited by
Violet Barungi and Hilda Twongyeirwe
FemRite Women Writers' Collective, Kampala

Introduction by
Rebecca Salonen

UnCUT/VOICES Press

ISBN: 978-3-9813863-5-6

Bibliographic information published by the Deutsche Nationalbibliothek.
The Deutsche Nationalbibliothek lists this publication in the Deutsche Nationalbibliografie; detailed bibliographic data are available on the Internet at http://dnb.d-nb.de
Frankfurt am Main: UnCUT/VOICES Press, 2015.

The cover painting, oil on canvas, is titled "Defiance" by Godfrey Williams-Okorodus, 2008.

This volume was originally published as Violet Barungi and Hilda Twongyeirwe, eds. *Beyond the Dance. Voices of Women on Female Genital Mutilation.*
FEMRITE PUBLICATIONS LIMITED
P.O. Box 705, Kampala
Tel: 256-041-543943/0772-743943
Email: info@femriteug.org
www.femriteug.org
Copyright © FEMRITE Uganda Women Writers Association 2009.
First Published 2009

About UnCUT/VOICES Press ...

Founded in Frankfurt am Main, Germany, UnCUT/VOICES Press is the first publisher to focus solely on female genital mutilation. By translating studies of FGM from French, German and other languages, UnCUT/VOICES Press broadens access to these indispensable resources. It also features significant and rare material in English aimed at ending an egregious injury still inflicted on African girls.

The founder Tobe Levin von Gleichen, a Visiting Research Fellow in International Gender Studies at Lady Margaret Hall, University of Oxford and an Associate of the Hutchins Center for African and African American Research at Harvard University, has been active against FGM since 1977. Co-editor with Augustine H. Asaah of *Empathy and Rage. Female Genital Mutilation in African Literature* (Ayebia, 2009), she served as founding president of FORWARD-Germany and has advised the Austrian Parliament, the Bundestag, Westminster, UNICEF and WHO. See also Levin, Tobe, ed. *Waging Empathy. Alice Walker,* Possessing the Secret of Joy *and the Global Movement to Ban FGM.* Frankfurt am Main: UnCUT/VOICES Press, 2014.

UnCUT/VOICES PRESS

Martin Luther Str. 35, 60389 Frankfurt am Main, Germany
Tobe.levin@uncutvoices.com www.uncutvoices.com
Geschäftsnummer HRB 86527, U.G. Haftungsbeschränkt

Also from UnCUT/VOICES Press

Khady with Marie-Thérèse Cuny. *Blood Stains. A Child of Africa Reclaims her Human Rights.* Trans. Tobe Levin. Frankfurt am Main: UnCUT/VOICES Press, 2010.

Prolongeau, Hubert. *Undoing FGM. Pierre Foldes, the Surgeon Who Restores the Clitoris.* Foreword Bernard Kouchner. Trans. and Afterword Tobe Levin. Frankfurt am Main: UnCUT/VOICES Press, 2011.

Mwaluko, Nick Hadikwa. *WAAFRIKA. 1992. Kenya. Two Women Fall in Love.* Frankfurt am Main: UnCUT/VOICES Press, 2013.

Hutton, Frankie, ed. *Rose Lore. Essays in Cultural History and Semiotics.* Frankfurt am Main: UnCUT/VOICES Press, 2015. With a chapter on FGM by Tobe Levin.

Kiminta Maria and Tobe Levin. *Kiminta. A Maasai's Fight against Female Genital Mutilation.* UnCUT/VOICES Press, 2015.

Table of Contents

Rebecca Salonen

Introduction

Even if you are involved in international female genital mutilation activism, you probably have not heard much about FGM in Uganda. Among the 28 African countries where female 'circumcision' is performed, Uganda stands near the bottom of the FGM-prevalence list, around 5% or less. This does not mean that female genital mutilation in Uganda is not a problem, but only that the Pokot, Tepeth, and Sabiny (Sebei), out of Uganda's 50-plus indigenous ethnic groups, practice FGM. These three groups live in remote and seasonally inaccessible regions on the eastern border with Kenya, where there are few casual visitors. Until recently, FGM was the lot of every girl in these societies, however, and the type of excision was very severe. Depending on the inspiration, ability, or eyesight of the circumciser, all of the external genitals are traditionally cut away. Most other Ugandans are horrified by the practice, and Parliament enacted the Prohibition of FGM act in 2010, so the public 'circumcision' ceremonies are disappearing, and the cutting is now being done secretly, in the dark.

I learned about female genital mutilation in Uganda almost by accident. In 1998, while I was visiting Kampala, a friend introduced me to Hon. Jane Frances Kuka, a Sabiny who was then Minister of Gender. She had famously escaped being circumcised by staying in school. When her opposition to the practice became too troublesome, in 1988 the elders bought rope and planned to tie her up and mutilate her by force. She escaped to Kampala and returned by helicopter with the Minister for Women, who suggested the elders give up compulsory FGM. Later, Hon. Kuka was elected to the women's seat for Kapchorwa in Parliament.

Hon. Kuka invited me to visit her home town of Kapchorwa during the 1998 'circumcision' season to attend Culture Day, a festival created by Uganda's Reproductive, Educative and Community Health (REACH) project which had been launched in 1996 by the United Nations Population Fund to combat female genital mutilation. In 1998, Uganda's president, Yoweri Museveni, arrived by helicopter at the mountaintop town. Standing in the bed of a truck, he delivered a speech to the thousands of Sabiny people gathered at the Boma Grounds for Culture Day, urging them to abandon their fiercely defended practice of female 'circumcision'. Others spoke as well, including leading elders, some of whom stood in front of the president and, to our surprise but apparently not to the president's, announced their determination to continue their traditional practices. Later that evening, visitors and Kapchorwa dignitaries gathered at a celebration dinner. After listening to some congratulatory speeches, a community leader rose. Looking squarely at the visitors, he said forcefully that theSabiny did not need anyone from New York or London to come to Kapchorwa and tell them what to do about female 'circumcision'.

That night, locked into our compound near Sipi, we lay awake in our beds hearing the sounds of 'circumcision' in the darkness: Feet marching on the roads, bells and whistles, singing and drumming that lasted all night long. At breakfast the next morning, as we looked out at the magnificent Sipi Falls plunging into the chasm below our lodge, our hosts told us how many girls had been cut at dawn. We wondered if any had died. The same ceremonies would continue for weeks, long after we had returned to our safe homes in the West. There was nothing we could have done. We were the people from New York and London whose views were irrelevant.

After returning home, a few of us formed the Godparents Association. We raised the funds to pay school fees for Sabiny girls (later also for Pokot girls, who are also at risk for 'circumcision') to help them stay in school and avoid being cut, as Hon. Kuka had done. Over the years, we have sponsored hundreds of girls in secondary schools, and a number have completed university studies and master's degrees. All of them have avoided FGM, defied cultural expectations, and taken new paths in life that do not require them to be cut. These are the young women who will help to transform their culture.

The book you are reading is a collection of the stories of girls and women who have firsthand knowledge about female 'circumcision' in Kapchorwa and elsewhere. Each story is valuable because it is authentic and unique. Although FGM is no longer the secret that once seemed unbelievable to people in the West, there are many hidden aspects that underlie the persistence of the practice. Some of these are revealed by the women who speak in these pages – witchcraft, coercion, intoxication. Unlike the young women we have sponsored, most of whom have hair-raising tales about escaping forced 'circumcision', many of the women in these pages (and even the circumcisers) did not have a choice and were forced into FGM.

We do not know exactly how many Ugandan women have suffered female genital mutilation or how many hundreds of girls are being cut every year. No census taker goes door to door in the mountains or pursues the migrating Pokot pastoralists to count the 'circumcised' women in their households. Eventually, once the aid funding is exhausted and the papers are written, the people from New York and London always go home. But the Sabiny will remain on Mt. Elgon, coping with the divisions and differences among them since their ancient practice became of interest to outsiders. Only they can stop female genital mutilation on the mountain.

Dorah Musiimire

Plucking a Rosebud

Have you ever plucked a rose bud?
At dawn when the dew is fresh
Forming round drops
On delicate chaste petals

Have you tried plucking a rose bud?
Youthful, strong, deeply set in her stalk
Waiting to blossom into a full flower
To spread wide the pride of her beauty

I have seen a rose bud
Ruthlessly extracted from her stalk
Forlorn with pain and shame
How villainous!

I have also witnessed
A crest fallen stalk
Decrying the fall of her bud
The epitome of her pride

But what's a rose tree
Without buds
For the pride of a rose
Lies in the beauty of her flowers

Betty Kituyi

Do not Count on Me

Amina Buraimu is a tall, sixty-something-looking woman with a stoop and a wrinkled face that seem to cover her past. She abandoned her culturally revered role as a circumciser of girls in 1996 when the REACH (Reproductive, Educative and Community Health) programme identified her as the most dangerous person ("Amina Atare") in the district and talked her out of it. She was considered dangerous because, as the most experienced circumciser in Kapchorwa, she was as swift as Moses Kipsiro, the Kapchorwa-born Olympic athlete, scampering from village to village, and from hill to hill in her red 'circumcision' dress, as if possessed, cutting an average of 100 girls in each village. According to what they said in the villages, if 'circumcision' is harmful, then she was the one who harmed the greatest number of girls.

"When our own women ministers from Sipi Sub-county, Kuka and Chokomondosi, stand up and speak against the cutting, who is Amina Braimu to continue doing it? They must be right when they say it is wrong because they have the experience," she reflects. The ministers said that the tradition of cutting girls to make them fully women is no longer acceptable or honourable. Amina was told that times have changed and, with them, so have a lot of the things once considered culturally important. New diseases like "slim" (HIV/AIDS) are killing the young before the old. The knife no longer makes girls "clean" as believed in the past but frequently transfers the AIDS virus. If one girl in the line has the virus and the same knife is used to cut all who follow her, the disease may be passed to everyone.

In Amina's time, girls were virgins when they were cut. Today, modern habits and practices lead many of them into having sex before marriage. It was also uncommon years ago to circumcise married women – they had all been cut before marriage – but now it is the trend. This is very risky, because in the Kapchorwa region the infection rates for sexually transmitted diseases are higher among married couples than among single people since many married people are not faithful to each other. The young women no longer keep the tribal secrets. Some circumcised women are now admitting they feel pain when they have sex with their husbands. When Amina was still a thin girl with a flat chest and her mother was breast-feeding her younger siblings, it was taboo to reveal what was going on in the bedroom. But now that people are talking, she acknowledged it could be true that 'circumcision' of girls is harmful.

****

Still, Amina relishes the memory of the days when she was the most skilful and powerful cutter in the land. She had a lot of money to spend and was able to afford almost anything she wanted. Circumcising girls earned her a lot of money and gifts from the girls' families. In fact, Amina was one of the richest women in her community. In a single 'circumcision' season, she would collect close to ten million shillings (about $5,000) as payment for her services. Her current circumstances, however, give no hint of her former wealth. As she talks, her sunken eyes and dry, cracked lips confirm her ill health, which she blames on the poverty that has attacked her like locusts on a cassava garden since she stopped excising girls. She tells me that she cannot afford any medicine and that her granaries have long been empty of maize and millet because she is too weak to tend the gardens and too poor to hire people to lend her a hand in cultivating them.

"Are you one of those government officials who always come to ask me about my experience?" Amina asks, patting my hand lightly. She continues, "Over the past few years, strange people from government have come here, driving their big vehicles, condemning the 'circumcision' of girls. They have tried to persuade me and my four colleagues to stop doing it. But only two of us have quit. Others still do it, deep in places like Bukwo. They are still circumcising -- for the money, especially. Look at me! I have nothing now! Those government people make promises that they never fulfil. Some people visited my home two years ago and promised to give me money to start a chicken-rearing project. They said they would build me a mabati, an iron-roofed house. But they have not honoured their promises, even though I told them that I did not have any other means of making a living."

As if her poverty had choked out any logical thought, Amina's sentiments seem to contradict the reasons she has earlier given for stopping her 'circumcision' of girls. She seems to say that she was forced to stop circumcising, and that if she does not get any other means of livelihood, she can very easily slip back into the practice of cutting girls.

"We do not like being held up in Paradise during the 'circumcision' period," she says. Paradise is a local hotel where the activists from REACH keep the circumcisers for a week in order to stop them from going out to cut the girls. "They tell us to relax and not to think about 'circumcision'. They promise to give us money to start projects, but they do not fulfil their promises," she says.

****

Like the hovering clouds in the Kapchorwa skies, Amina's moods shift. She seems to brighten again when she tells me how she became a circumciser. It turns out that she never wanted to become one at all. As a young girl, she had heard stories of girls who bled to death after they were badly cut. She did not want to shoulder the blame if such an accident happened. She resisted becoming a circumciser for twenty years, but finally gave in after 'circumcision' spirits tortured her with sickness.

"In those days," she begins, "one became a circumciser through a special calling from Ayuik, the 'circumcision' spirits. The gift to circumcise ran in families from one generation to the next: a grandmother who was a circumciser could pass on the tools of 'circumcision' to her granddaughter if Ayuik identified her and gave her the knowledge of the knife."

"When Ayuik found a suitable candidate," she continued, "they possessed her, took over her mind, and made her act with supernatural powers, doing unbelievable things like being able to walk on the edge of a cliff without falling, or to sense danger. The one chosen by the spirits could even sleep in the deep caves, sharing them with snakes and wild animals, and come out unharmed."

For Amina, one thing led to another. She was naturally a sickly child. At fourteen, when no traditional herbs or white man's medicine could cure her of the ailments that ate the flesh off her bones and left her thin like one of the cassava stems in her mother's garden, the elders suspected her to be suffering because of the 'circumcision' spirits. In those days, whenever a young girl had some mysterious sickness and became too thin, 'circumcision' was often considered the cure. The elders decided to cut Amina.

"I was circumcised by a very old woman who came to the inner room where I lay. She was carried on a man's back. When he put her down, I saw that she could not stand without support." Amina pats her brow as if to smooth away a headache before she tells me more. "Because I was too ill, I could not sing and dance with the other girls. I fainted and slipped into a coma. I woke up five days later hearing the murmurs of a witch doctor who had been summoned from the Kalenjins in Kenya to treat me. With deep groans, then in a frightening shriek, the witch doctor announced that I had special powers and prophesied that I would circumcise very many girls when the right time came."

Now that she was believed to have the special abilities of a circumciser and was destined to be a custodian of the ancestral Sabiny knowledge, Amina's health improved, and she even put some flesh on her bony frame. With these powers, she was no ordinary young woman, and she was more attractive to men, many of whom sought to marry her.

As was not unexpected for a newly cut woman, especially one of Amina's calibre, she was accosted one day when she was on her way from the well. "I was balancing a big water pot on my head and walking without a care toward home when suddenly I heard heavy footsteps behind me. I turned and saw a man I had never seen before. He grabbed my pot and put it down. He then picked me up and carried me on his shoulders like a banana stem. I tried to scream, but he covered my mouth with his hand and ordered me to keep quiet because he was now my husband. After we had moved a good distance from my home, the man put me down. Holding my hand firmly, he led me to his hut. That is how I became his wife. My parents never looked for me, but they got to know through rumours what had happened. Eventually, this man went to them and told them of his intention to marry me. He paid the bride price, and I became his wife officially."

Five years of marriage brought Amina some wealth but no children. Her husband and mother-in-law caused her sleepless nights because she failed to bear them children. Amina slipped into a depression, and soon she was in the world of spirits. What was left of her private parts began itching. When that happened, her grand-mother said, it meant female spirits were attacking her. This was yet another confirmation that she was to become a circumciser.

"Later," she narrates, "I heard three women's voices within me. They were saying that they would kill me if I did not want to circumcise the girls. I heard the voices whenever I put my head down to sleep. I fled from them and tried to hide in the forest. But when it grew dark and the owls began crying two-whee-two-whee in the foliage above me, I knew I was a dead woman, and I ran back home. There is a Sabiny belief around the crying of owls: when they cry in the village, someone dies."

"One day," she went on, "I heard the women's voices in my head in broad daylight. Their voices were louder than the village gramo-phone. They were saying, 'Hold the knife of your grandmother.' My head became very hot. I felt a strong urge to stand under the water-fall to soothe my head and have the swishing rush of the water drown out the spirits' voices. I began to run at breakneck speed to-wards Cheptui River Falls. My husband ran after me and tried to stop me, but as fast as an antelope fleeing a hungry lion I ran into the deep pool where the water plunges into a hole several metres deep. When I did not come up again, my husband thought that I was dead, and he called for help."

"I don't remember anything that took place while I was under the water, but I remember that I was brought to the surface by my hus-band and panic-stricken villagers. To everyone's amazement, I had jingles on my ankles and wrists when I came out of the water. This was surprising because I did not have the bells when I entered the water. Suddenly, as I was being led home by my husband, I felt well. The jingles on my feet made the hunting dog's sound, attracting people to pop out of their houses like white ants emerging after a light evening rain."

As Amina talks, I ask more questions, but she is not willing to be diverted from her story. With a lot of reservations, I continue to listen.

"My husband took me to my parents' home in Kibanda village, in Kwoti Sub-county, on the northern slope of Mount Elgon. For my parents and the elders, the appearance of the jingles was further confirmation that I was destined to be a circumciser. They decided immediately to summon my old grandmother, who was also a circumciser, to hand me the tools so that I could begin cutting girls."

"The tool-giving ceremony was an interesting ritual. A goat was slaughtered for a feast. The tools my grandmother passed on included two new knives made from nails hammered flat, which were tied to my hands; a whetstone (lutetyo) made out of cement, for sharpening the knives; millet flour for rubbing onto the girls' private parts to make them rough and easy to grip; and a short-sleeved red gown marked with a danger sign painted in white. Special alcoholic drinks of millet (komeka baka) and maize (komeka teshonik) were spat on my face by my grandmother, after which she declared me a circumciser."

Amina Buraimu did not begin to circumcise immediately because she was still scared. One day, as the 'circumcision' season approached, some spirits called her by name in a dream. Between 4 and 5 a.m. they called, "Amina, Amina, why do you refuse to circumcise the girls?" The spirits promised to stand with her, make her brave, and teach her. They would give her the knowledge.

They also threatened that if she refused they would kill her.

"The following morning," she recounts, "I heard whistles outside my father's hut, and by the time I came out, three girls were dancing vigorously in the yard, accompanied by an excited crowd of women, young and old. When they saw me, they bowed and fell on their knees. In song, they told me that they had come to fetch my knife, as they had chosen me to circumcise them. By custom, that is how it is done. The girls fetch the knife from the circumciser a day before they are to be cut, and when she gives it to them they take it as a sign of commitment. The girls return home to prepare for the rest of the ceremony."

"I remember quite vividly the first girl I cut. I was very frightened. It was in 1978, and I was thirty years old. First, I prayed to the women spirits for wisdom and strength. Immediately afterwards, I swiftly cut off the girl's clitoris. Then I ran away and hid in the bushes because I thought I had not done the excision properly. As is the practice, the mentors picked up my knife and threw the excised clitoris into the pit latrine."

But true to their word, the 'circumcision' spirits guided Amina as she carried out subsequent 'circumcisions' over the next ten years.

She became very competent with the knife. All the girls she has cut regard her as a godmother, and she is often called on to give advice to them and their families.

I asked Amina whether she had passed on her special abilities to anybody else, and she said that she believed it was not within her power to do so. No one in her lineage had shown signs like those that she had experienced prior to being initiated into the practice.

*****

Amina sees her abandonment of the practice in 1996 as an inspiration to the other circumcisers, who followed her example. She would like to be rewarded for leading others out of the profession. Some of her fellow circumcisers were also persuaded by REACH to give up circumcising, and they were given gifts of cows.

Amina has been married for thirty years but has no children. She left her husband and now lives alone. Her husband married a second woman who bore him children. I asked whether her being unable to bear children was associated with her having been circumcised, but she dismissed the question, saying that that would take us into another story, which she said she would not want to tell. However, she said that she had learned that genital mutilation could be the cause of her infertility, though it was too late to change matters now.

"In the past, such information was not available because no one complained and no one found out. But with the anti-FGM campaigns that condemn the practice, I believe they have talked to the people and the truth is now known."

One cannot help wondering why the spirits who had started Amina's cutting career in the first place did not object to her quitting.

Before I part ways with Amina, I want to ask her where she thinks the jingles on her ankles and wrists came from. I am tempted to think it was a trick, but I don't tell her that.

Her final words about FGM underscore her belief that only education can wipe it out, can empower the girls to be serious and to ask questions about their lives. She appeals to the government to assist her to start some income-generating activities so that she can have a new livelihood. To all those girls intending to get circumcised she says, "Do not wriggle your waists counting on me, because I am no longer a circumciser."

Jemeo Nanyonjo

Tonight

Tonight is my maiden ceremony
Having gone through the thin sieve of initiation,
I have five girls to bring into womanhood.
Tonight I blunt their sensitivity with my sharp knife
Having experienced what I shall take them through,
I have to smile through their pain.
Tonight is my maiden ceremony

I search my first victim's face
Do I seek fear, pride, anger or bravery?
I search my memory of experience
To remember the atmosphere of that very evening
To remember the look on the faces of the women I represent
To remember the response of my waiting tensed teenage body
To remember the after-feel of that very ceremony
My mind is a blank!

I search my first victim's face
Something glitters in her pupils
A coded message I fail to decode
My confidence slips away
My hands start to tremble
My eyes become teary
My legs wobble
My brain becomes weary
I step aside.

Shall the burdens of the girls I have failed to bring
into womanhood forever follow me?

Grace Atuhaire

I am already a woman!

I rose
Surrounded by clansmen
With spears and knives
'Make her a woman!'

I froze
At the sound of the knives assembled
Smeared in white sand
'Make her a woman!'

I shuddered
At mum's consent
At the indifferent strangers
'Make her a woman!'

I fled!
And stood for what was right
Ignorance makes no woman
I am already a woman!

Bananuka Jocelyn Ekochu

The Woman in Me

Eight kilometres from Kapchorwa town, along the Kapchorwa-Mbale Road, a woman is busy preparing lunch for her family in a rough kitchen that cannot accommodate the fireplace and cook at the same time. At forty-seven, Judith can easily be mistaken for sixty. A couple of metres from the kitchen is a small grass-thatched mud-and-wattle hut. This is the family home. A peek inside reveals a smooth floor of mud and cow dung, nothing else. A wall separates the sitting area from what must be the bedroom.

The place is just a few kilometres from the famous Sipi Falls, the tourist attraction on Mount Elgon. The upper falls is a spectacular set of twins cascading down as if in some kind of competition, while the powerful lower falls roars with such rage that viewers keep a respectful distance as they watch, in fascination, the sparkling flying waters.

It has just rained, and Judith's compound is soggy. She sits at the entrance of her kitchen, which spits out smoke that mercilessly attacks her eyes. Every now and then she wipes away a tear with the back of her hand. Her head, wrapped in a scarf of undefined colour, is covered by ash, courtesy of the stubborn fire, which, owing to the weather, is not easy to keep ablaze. Judith has to keep blowing at it to make sure that it continues burning.

On the higher side of the hut, scattered in the grass, are plastic plates and cups, and saucepans blackened by soot, waiting to be washed. An eight-year-old girl approaches to do just that. She is the daughter of Judith's sister. The girl originally came to help Judith with domestic chores, but now that her mother is dead she has to continue living with Judith's family.

"She is now mine, and she helps me with the work when she comes back from school," Judith says. Judith feels guilty. She thinks that as the woman of the house she should be the one doing all the work, but she cannot. Her niece is very young and should not be working as hard as she is, but there is simply nothing that can be done about it.

On the lower side of the hut, near the door, an old woman sits shelling fresh beans. They make a beautiful mix of colours as she casually tosses them into a wide basket. Some are pink, some are white, but most of them are maroon. The woman is Judith's friend, who once in a while comes to help her out with any work that needs to be done. On seeing us, the woman gets up with the kind of agility that makes one wonder about her age. Her face reads seventy or more; her swiftness points to fifty. Her face is wreathed in a smile as she greets us and starts speaking very rapidly in Kupsabiny. She must be a very jolly soul, we think. After a short while, she seems to lose interest in us and goes back to her beans.

Across the road a lone cow is feeding from a wooden trough. Next to it, a young man is busy cutting a banana stem into pieces. He chops with the speed of an angry butcher, while the cow, as if trying to slow him down, eats with the grace of a satisfied zebra. He sprinkles salt onto the pieces and adds them to the ones in the trough. The cow continues to feed, not allowing the replenishment to break its rhythm.

A few metres away, a woman is washing clothes in a ditch at the roadside. There is no tap and she has no jerry can or any other container apart from the basin in which she is doing her washing. A closer look reveals that the water she is using flows from underground.

"You are welcome," Judith says to us, in a typical local greeting.

Her son, about twenty-two years old, brings us seats in a show of hospitality – one wooden folding chair, a piece of flattened wood, and a metal chair with plastic strings, half of them lost to old age. He places a seat in front of each of us, shaking them a bit to make sure that they are firm on the ground. Not until we have made ourselves as comfortable as we can does he open his mouth to speak.

"You are welcome." He echoes his mother's greeting, hovering around her in an impressively protective manner. He finally finds himself a comfortable spot to squat on the veranda of the hut. He then fixes his eyes on us, his heavy eyeglasses giving him a fierce look. His manner clearly says, "You upset my mother and you will have me to contend with." Many strangers, it turns out, have been coming to listen to Judith's story. It is not a story that she enjoys telling, and sometimes she gets upset.

An official from REACH, the anti-FGM NGO in Kapchorwa, explains the purpose of our visit, first convincing Judith's son that we are harmless, and then persuading her to tell her story.

"My English is bad," she says shyly. "I stopped in Primary Six."

Actually, I think her English is quite good, considering the time she has spent out of school, in a village where English is not always spoken. In Primary Six she would have been eleven or twelve years old. That is thirty-five or more years ago. In addition, at the time she went to school, 1967 to 1973, in rural schools English was taught using the vernacular. For Judith to remember enough of it to sustain a conversation is impressive.

Eight-year-old Miracle, the youngest of Judith's five children, all of them boys, plants himself at her side. He looks at us suspiciously, but does not say anything. His first smile appears when his mother explains the reason for his name. When he smiles one sees how handsome he is. His white teeth light up his dark-skinned face. It is obvious that he will grow into a tall man. As if realising that all eyes are on him, he shyly turns and faces the other way.

"His birth was a miracle," Judith explains. "Nobody thought I would ever be pregnant again, and when it happened, nobody believed I would carry the pregnancy to full term, let alone deliver the baby." She has a reflective look on her face as she says. "The woman in me died at the hands of the circumciser."

Judith's husband, a quiet, healthy-looking dark-skinned man, doesn't say a word. He moves around with a few freshly picked coffee beans in a transparent polythene bag. One has to remember that Judith is only forty-seven years old in order not to mistake her husband for one of her five sons. Finally he enters the hut, comes out with a camera slung over his shoulder, and disappears down the road. A small-time photographer, he saunters around the village in search of people who may want to have their pictures taken.

****

Judith is one of the thousands of female genital mutilation victims in the area. Together with her cousin Monica and their friend Betty, she was subjected to the knife in 1976. She was sixteen years old then. The three girls were born in a village called Arokwo, which is in Tegeres Sub-county, Tingey County, then Kapchorwa District.

"I didn't think much about it, but my family felt I should be circumcised and pressured me into having it done. And, of course, at the time I also wanted to get married. In those days, unless a woman was circumcised, she could not get married. She was treated as a child but without the love that is usually accorded children. She would be subjected to all sorts of ridicule, and, finally, she would be circumcised by force. 'Circumcision' was not something a woman chose to do -- it was what she had to do."

Judith craved the respect given to circumcised women and never thought about the consequences of the practice. She was led to believe that the pain was the same as the pain of childbirth, which passes and is quickly replaced by the joy of the baby. She believed that joy would come in the form of marriage. She would have a husband, children, and a home of her own.

On that fateful day in December 1976, at sixteen and nineteen years old, respectively, Judith and Monica were collected to be circumcised, taken from their homes under escort by their relatives and other members of the community. Their friend Betty, who was employed as a nurse at Kapchorwa Hospital at the time, was on night duty. When she learned about the plan to circumcise her by force, she tried to hide. Unfortunately, when Betty's relatives came looking for her, her fellow staff members and the patients at the hospital revealed her hiding place. She was pulled out, tied up, and dragged to where her two friends were being held.

"We were made to dance the whole night. The bystanders kept insulting us. At one time, we were taken inside a hut and trained to become witches," Judith says in her soft voice, shaking her head as if wondering how she could have gone through with it.

So why should they be trained in witchcraft? What does it have to do with being initiated into adulthood? Must one become a witch in order to be considered a full woman? I was curious.

"They taught us how to bewitch any woman who misbehaved," she answers. However, Judith still will not tell anybody, not even her closest relatives, the details of the training. Whatever the girls were told to do to become witches cannot be revealed.

"They told us that if we revealed the details, they would know, and then we would be punished severely, probably by death. I can't tell you." Judith explains that at dawn the following morning, they were taken to a kraal in Kapchorwa town, seized and held down as the "surgeon" took their womanhood away. Monica was the first one to be cut because her father was older. She was followed by Betty, and Judith came last.

There were no painkillers for them. A woman was expected to look after herself and not to complain about petty things like pain. The exercise seemingly went as planned, and there were no immediate complications. The girls walked four kilometres to the traditional recovery hut, where a number of rituals were performed. Most of these they are not allowed to disclose, but rumours are that a leopard scratches four marks on the circumcised girls' right arms, a sign of their initiation.

The girls spent a week in the one-room grass-thatched seclusion hut. There were no mats or mattresses. Nobody was allowed to sleep on a mattress until she had bathed and was clean. And nobody was allowed to bathe until her bleeding stopped. The girls were therefore made to sleep for a week on a hard earthen floor covered with leaves.

"The mentors – women who had been circumcised in previous years and were considered exemplary – were supposed to help us by washing our wounds, but in most cases they did not. They did take the severed genital parts away with them. Instead of disposing of them, they would use the flesh to bewitch anyone who did not pay them. If the mentors bewitched you using your private parts, you would neither get married nor have children. That is how they made sure that everybody paid," Judith tells us.

She says the mentors never monitored the healing process of the girls, but they often checked to see if any part of their genitals remained. If so, they would call the circumcisers to complete the job.

Even though the girls were not completely healed, after one week they left the traditional nursing hut and went home to prepare for the passing-out-of-seclusion ceremony, known as yotunetap cemerik. Many additional rituals were performed during the passing-out ceremony.

Judith's wound healed, but she started to feel numb in her legs once in a while. It was not such a serious problem at first, and it did not bother her much. After all, she was now a complete woman and no longer a girl. She was fit to be a wife. As a young girl she had looked forward to the day she would get married and have children and a home of her own.

Judith realised part of her dream one year after 'circumcision', in 1977, when she found herself a husband. When she became pregnant and then gave birth to a baby boy, her joy was complete. She consented to sex out of a sense of duty to her husband, but she never enjoyed it at all. "Not even once!" she says. Still, there was some strangely agreeable feeling that came out of the pain she had to endure every time she gave in to him.

"And I was very happy when I had my first child, and everything seemed okay. But the numbness in my legs was becoming more frequent than before," she says, recalling the beginning of her suffering.

****

In the meantime, the two girls with whom Judith had faced the knife, Monica and Betty, were going through similar experiences. Unexplained sensations in their legs progressed into numbness. Three years later, they were all complaining of pain in the knees and around the waist, especially after walking long distances. After heavy work, they would suffer general body pains. By 1987, eleven years after their 'circumcision', the three women could no longer walk without help. They had to use crutches or walking sticks, or lean on another person for support.

"After I had my third child, my legs became very weak. Every time I tried to walk I would fall," Judith explains. She visited many clinics and saw many doctors, but nobody could diagnose her condition. Betty and Monica also visited numerous doctors, but found no help. Because no one could diagnose their illness, no medicine could be prescribed.

"Every doctor I saw told me that there was nothing wrong with me. I even went to Mulago and Nsambya, the big hospitals in Kampala, where I had my fourth child. But they could not find anything." The puzzled look on her face says it all.

At this time Uganda was just recovering from the effects of a five-year civil war and had only minimal medical services. However, Betty had a brother who was working in Kenya. In 1987 he arranged for her to be taken to Kenyatta Hospital, in Nairobi, where there were better facilities. But even the best doctors with the best facilities in Kenya could not give a clear diagnosis. All they could do for Betty was give her painkillers.

In 1992 Monica had begun developing numbness in her legs, and by 1997 she was paralysed. She too had visited several health centres and private clinics, to no avail. The mysterious numbness progressed relentlessly. As is always the case in rural areas in Uganda, any sickness that cannot be explained by doctors is attributed to witchcraft. Judith and her friends were therefore advised to seek the intervention of a witchdoctor.

"Every witchdoctor we visited told us that we were bewitched by the circumciser. We did not understand why she would have done this to us since we paid her fully," Judith muses. Her gaze shifts to a donkey struggling up the road, weighed down by a load of cabbages.

The women decided to confront the circumciser. "She did not deny our allegations. She just said that we should pay her more to remove the curse. Although we did not know why she had cursed us, we went ahead and paid her – whatever she asked for, including a cow. We only wanted to be healed." They were willing to do anything to be able to walk again.

After they had paid their supposed tormentor, they sat and waited for her to remove the curse. They fully expected to be healed and to return to normal lives. After all, the person who they believed had caused their suffering was willing to undo the damage. But this did not happen.

"She did not remove the curse," Judith says sadly. "We heard that the mentors had advised the circumciser not to remove it. They told her that if she took away the curse, she would be admitting that she had bewitched us in the first place, and our families would kill her because we had suffered so much already."

Now Judith believes that it was all hogwash.

"I think she did not do her job properly. Something in our bodies must have been damaged when she circumcised us. Maybe she cut the wrong place," she reasons.

The women continued looking for a medical solution to their strange disorder. Then, at the beginning of 2000, all three women developed a skin rash that covered their bodies and was especially intense during the wet season. The rash would respond to medication and would generally disappear when the dry season started. Later, the rash grew worse and developed into sores affecting the lower parts of the body, from the waist down to the toes. Monica, who was the first to be cut, had the most severe rash, followed by Betty. For Judith, who had been the last cut, the rash was mild. No one knew why it was so. Perhaps whatever caused the rash had something to do with the knife that was used to cut the three women.

By December 2005 Monica was bedridden and suffering from bedsores. She was admitted to Kapchorwa Hospital in January 2006, complaining of abdominal pains, vomiting, and diarrhea. She was very weak, and her body was generally wasted. She was treated with antibiotics, analgesics, and other forms of supportive therapy while tests were done to check for abnormalities or signs of infection. All findings were basically negative, except that Monica was dangerously anemic, perhaps because of persistent ill health and her resulting poor appetite. She had to be given blood transfusions on several occasions. Her extensive bedsores were severe, despite the treatment she was receiving, and she had to have surgical debridement of the wounds. By the next year, her sores had become septic. Monica's health continued to deteriorate, and when she contracted malaria in April 2008, her immune system was unable to withstand it, even with treatment. At the end of the month, Monica lost the fight and passed away, having battled sickness for close to thirty years. She was fifty years old when she died.

Betty went through similar bad-health experiences. She also suffered paralysis, skin rashes, and bedsores. In addition, she developed high blood pressure and needed continuous treatment. Betty was a staunch Christian, an Anglican. When she became disabled, a friend introduced her to the Perfection Church Ministries which began supporting her financially. Betty lived by faith and was hopeful about a bright future. After the death of her friend Monica, she embarked on a regime of prayer and fasting, seeking God's intervention in a fight that she no longer understood.

Shortly after she started fasting, she experienced severe abdominal pain and was admitted to Kapchorwa Hospital for treatment. Soon after her hospitalisation, Betty suffered a stroke and her condition worsened. The medical team did all they could, but it was clear she needed more advanced facilities. She was referred to Mulago Hospital in Kampala, and an ambulance was provided for her transportation. A few kilometres before she reached Mulago, Betty breathed her last. She was fifty-three years old when she died.

****

According to REACH, the cause of the three women's paraplegia, and Monica's and Betty's deaths, cannot be explained medically. But the women and their relatives firmly believe that their ill health resulted from the female genital mutilation they suffered.

The local people also talk. When it was time for the 'circumcision' dues to be paid, they say, the father of one of the girls was drunk. For some reason, he supposedly poured hot water on the circumciser and the child she was carrying on her back. This humiliation angered her so much that she cursed the girls she had cut. Others say that there was competition between two groups of mentors who were supposed to perform the girls' passing-out ceremonies. The group that was left out is believed to have cursed the operation because they lost their fees. Another possibility is that during the cutting, some veins and nerves were simply damaged accidentally.

REACH officials have called for further medical research into the disorder that affected these women. Those things had never occurred before in the Sabiny community. Of course, cases of hemorrhage and shock, sometimes leading to death, had been reported after circumcisions, but prolonged sickness leading to disability and then death had never been seen before.

Judith, the only surviving member of the trio, is permanently crippled and fears that she, too, might soon follow her friend and her cousin. She has a wheelchair, but it is inconvenient to use at home. She cannot, for example, cook comfortably in a wheelchair. If she tried to reach down from the chair into the cooking fire, she would risk falling into the flames. She therefore uses two small pieces of wood to pull herself around on the ground, sitting on one and pushing the other in front of her. Supporting herself with her hands, she hauls herself forward and sits on the front piece, reaches behind her to pick up the rear piece, pushes it forward, and repeats the exercise laboriously until she gets to her destination.

Once it was evident that nothing could be done to reverse the damage that had disabled Judith, her husband packed his bags and left. He had no use for a crippled wife. It did not seem to matter that she had given him the best of her life, including four children at the time.

The story of what happened to Judith, Monica, and Betty has travelled far and wide. People have come from all over Uganda and beyond to listen to Judith recount it. When her husband abandoned her, REACH gave Judith a million shillings (about $500), to set up a small business. She opened a small roadside shop selling essential commodities like soap, salt, and kerosene. One day, as Judith sat waiting for customers, a shadow fell over her. She raised her eyes, expecting to see a customer, but – lo and behold! -- there was her husband, larger than life, looking pleased with himself. He had come home. Shortly after this, Judith found she was pregnant, and later she delivered Miracle. Nobody had expected this to happen, given the state of her health and the fact that she was severely disabled.

****

As we prepare to leave, in a show of generosity Judith instructs her son to pack up the fresh beans her friend had shelled. Putting them in a polythene bag, Miracle hands the beans to my friend, who accepts them as a blessing.

After this small, touching example of friendship, I cannot help wondering how a place can contain such contradictions. But Kapchorwa is a puzzling place. It is endowed with the kind of natural beauty that leaves one breathless, and its friendly people are generous with their time and resources. Yet at the same time, Kapchorwa is plagued with the devastating practice of female genital mutilation. It does not seem to matter to its adherents that it has led to death and disability. A good number of Sabiny people have come out strongly against it, but there are also those who still insist that it is a tradition that must be maintained.

Perhaps the most disturbing aspect of this practice is the secrecy surrounding the actual rituals performed. Any woman who has been circumcised, even if she has come to denounce it, will tell you that she can never reveal these rituals, the ancient secrets of her tribe.

Lindah Niwenyesiga

Sacrilege

I weep
Tears of repulsive colours
Because you wrecked the bulwarks
That fuelled my blazing desire
Your implacable cultural measures
Have splashed into a zillion scourges

Linda Lilian

All for Tradition

All for tradition
My pride to rid
A hollow edition
Of me
My ride to reel

What is taken is forsaken
The crimson feels not a token
All for tradition
Treading to that myth
Tried for risk

No gain more pain
More vain
This slit silted
The fake manhood
My bloodhood
This my tradition
Wills my fever
Not the fervour

Sharon Lamwaka and Hilda Twongyeirwe Rutagonya

Petals for the Wind

It is a Saturday morning. As we approach Hanifa, she does not seem to acknowledge our arrival. She sits quietly at the gate of the offices of the African Centre for Treatment and Rehabilitation of Torture Victims (ACTV), a non-governmental organisation that provides medical treatment to torture victims in Uganda and the neighbouring countries in the Great Lakes region. The organisation also advocates against torture in an effort to prevent its occurrence.

Hanifa is a very striking young woman. Locks of shiny dark hair dangle at the sides of her face, escaping from the black-and-white scarf around her head and neck. She glances at us very briefly and then looks away again. We are not quite sure how to start the interview on our prickly topic.

When we greet Hanifa, she responds cheerfully although her eyes do not quite meet ours. We are encouraged by the warmth in her voice. We invite her to the FEMRITE offices in Kamwokya, Kampala, and she gets into the vehicle with us. We ride off chitchatting about nothing in particular. At FEMRITE we offer her a cup of tea. She does not readily accept it. Nevertheless, we set the tea in front of us and sip from our own cups. We are still not sure how to begin and, as if she is reading our minds, she clears her throat and smiles.

"Faith says you would like to talk to me about female 'circumcision'." Faith is the woman who arranged our meeting with Hanifa.

"Yes, yes!" we respond enthusiastically.

"That is not a problem, but I will tell you my story on one condition," she begins.

We are suspicious of her condition. We are taken by surprise by the sudden appearance of her confidence and strength.

"One condition?" we ask.

"Yes, or maybe two."

"Let's hear them, then."

We do not want to linger over any unspoken conditions. We smile and encourage her to speak.

"I will share my story on condition that you will avail it to the rest of the world so that it can eventually help other women not to undergo the pain that I went through and still go through. Secondly, I would like to keep my identity undisclosed because 'circumcision' is such a demeaning experience that no woman would want people to know that she is circumcised."

With our eyes we make a silent agreement, and Hanifa proceeds to tell us her story.

"I was born in Ethiopia in a town called Mega. My father is an Ethiopian, and my mother is a Somali. I have no idea where the two of them met, but they are husband and wife. I have six sisters and five brothers, and all of us were born in Mega town in Ethiopia. I am the third-born in the family. It is very unfortunate, however, that I do not remember anything about my childhood with my parents and my siblings.

"I do not know how old I was when my mother's sister came to our home and requested my mother to give her a child that would become her daughter. My aunt had given birth to six sons, and she desperately wanted a daughter who would help her, especially with domestic chores around the house. Because my mother had several daughters, she agreed to donate one, and the donation was me. I have not found the heart to forgive my parents for entering into such an arrangement. My mother says that it is common in Somalia for families to share children, but my father says that he agreed to it only because he did not want to antagonise my mother. I find both explanations unconvincing.

"My father is from the Oromo tribe, one of the smallest tribes in Ethiopia. The Oromo traditions regarding women are not very different from the Somali ones. In most Ethiopian customs, just as in Somalia, women do not have rights equal to those of men. For example, in the Oromo culture, men dictate how women should behave and sometimes how they dress. Men eat first while women wait upon them. A woman does not openly talk about the man she has fallen in love with because it is the brothers or fathers who approve and recommend husbands. Arranged marriages are still very common in Ethiopia and, indeed, in Somalia. But comparatively, Ethiopians respect women more than Somalis do. In the Oromo tribe women are not circumcised.

"Due to war and insecurity in Ethiopia and Somalia, many people have relocated to other countries, all over the world. For the same reason my aunt, with her Somali husband, relocated to Kenya – to

Mweyale village, at the border with Ethiopia. That is where my aunt took me, and that is where I grew up, believing that the family in Mweyale was my biological family. My aunt was my mother, and her husband was my father. They had six boys who were my cousins, but also my brothers. And there was not a single day when any of them made me doubt I belonged there. It never crossed my mind that my aunt might not be my mother.

"In Mweyale, I was taken to Mweyale Primary School, where my cousins-brothers also studied. Life was normal until sometime when I was in Primary Three. One morning my aunt called me and told me to bathe and be very clean. I don't remember which holiday it was, I only vaguely remember that I was in Primary Three and that it was holiday time. She said that she wanted to take me to visit her friend in a nearby village. She gave me my best clothes to wear, and I was very happy. I always enjoyed going visiting with her because it made me feel very special, especially whenever we left the boys behind.

"We set off very early in the morning. We walked a short distance, and I was surprised that I did not recognize the homestead at which our journey stopped. This dampened my excitement a bit, but I was happy to find two other girls were there also, with their mothers. Before we could talk and get to know each other, we were taken straight to an empty hut in the homestead.

"All the mothers stayed outside while we girls, accompanied by three other women, walked into a bare room. I found this a bit strange, and yet I never suspected what they were going to do to us. I was reassured by the thought at the back of my mind that, since my mother had brought me there, nothing harmful was going to happen to me. One of the girls, who was older than us, was grumbling all along, though she did not say anything openly. She just looked at everyone suspiciously, her eyes moving from one woman to the other. As for the other two of us, we giggled and wondered why she was being so difficult and disrespectful.

"When we got into the room, the women sat us down and told us that we were now being prepared for chastity. 'From today onwards, you should never sleep with any man until your wedding night. If you do it, we shall know and all your people will know because your virginity will be broken,' the women told us.

"As they talked to us, I remembered that my aunt-mother had also mentioned to me something about not sleeping with men until my marriage. 'What we are about to do today is to protect you and to keep you chaste,' one of the women continued.

"I had vaguely heard about virginity, and so I thought that these women were going to give us virginity. I thought that this older girl who was grumbling was afraid of getting her virginity from these women. I thought that perhaps she was not a good girl and that she knew she would not protect hers till marriage. But of course I never said anything. For myself, I was ready not to shame my parents and brothers, and so I was eager to receive my virginity and to protect it till my marriage. But I must admit that all these concepts were very vague in my mind. Only much, much later in life did I realise that this girl must have known what they were going to do to us.

"The preparation talk took a couple of minutes, and then we were told to sit on the floor. I do not quite remember what happened after that, except that suddenly the three women pounced on me. One mountain of a woman quickly took a position behind me and thrust her legs around me and between mine, forcing my legs wide apart. At the same time, she pinned my arms tightly against my stomach. The second woman quickly blindfolded me. I felt an awkward shuffle between my legs and then a sharp pain that felt like hot pepper in a wound. The blindfold was removed as fast as it had been put on, and then the mountain-woman let go of my arms and legs.

"When I looked around, I did not see anyone. The two girls were still there. The women were there. But I saw none of them. All I could see was the pool of blood that surrounded me. There was so much blood that the women were scooping it up with cupped hands and pouring it into basins. I screamed – not because of the pain but because of the shock of seeing the blood that threatened to form a lake around my body. For a moment, it seemed as if I were going to drown in my own blood. I even remember that my aunt-mother appeared at the door, and she too let out a scream. 'My God, what have you done to my daughter? That is too much blood. That is not normal,' she said. But they shushed her into silence.

"I must have been the first one to be cut, but I do not remember seeing the other girls being cut. I was too shocked to think about the others -- too shocked to look beyond my own blood. In addition, everything happened so fast that I did not have time to reflect about anything.

"The women poured a reddish, gummy herb on the cut area to close the wound. Then they tied my legs together, one rope round my ankles and another round my thighs. I heard them say that the ropes would keep my legs in position. As the shock wore off, the women held me up and started to pour tepid water over me to wash the blood off my legs and groin. I realised that the other two girls were also being held up and washed. They too were in ropes. A sorry sight we were, if you ask me! We were all done and finished within minutes. Incidentally, I don't remember seeing many razor blades. I vaguely remember seeing one woman holding one. The room was cleaned spotless, and fresh mattresses were spread for us on the floor. For three weeks we stayed in that room with our legs tied together. When we needed to urinate, we would just stand and let the urine run down our legs, holding our breaths and shivering with the almost unbearable pain.

"Every single day for three weeks, the big girl complained. She quarrelled with the women all the time. In the evenings, our mothers would attend to us, sleeping in our newly acquired room by turns. The big girl quarrelled with her mother whenever she came, and even refused to eat the food she brought. It was funny that the girl never talked to us about why she was complaining. She just looked through us as if we did not exist. I was very sure that I wanted to grumble too because of the pain I was going through, though at the same time I was grateful to these women for having given me virginity.

"And all I wanted now was to keep that damned virginity in order to win the respect of my husband-to-be and to give my family the pride they deserved. I had no idea at all that I was already a virgin before these women did what they did with my budding femininity."

Hanifa did not know then that what they had just done was to make her suited to a man's desires, a sex machine with no feelings of her own, an object of pride and pleasure for others. The women had taken advantage of her innocence to confuse her and rob her of her womanhood, her future self.

"Now I know that the big girl already understood issues of sexuality," Hanifa continues. "She was so disturbed that she left our house of seclusion as soon as we were untied at the end of the three weeks. The other girl and I stayed for a few more days, during which we were taught how to walk and sit with our legs tightly closed. 'If you open your legs wide, your womanhood will open and that will affect your virginity!' The warning was always the same.

"We did not stay long after the big girl had left. Our mothers came for us and took us back home. My parents bought me new clothes and a bigger mattress. I don't remember being excited the way I used to be whenever I got new things. This time my feelings were dull, as blunted as they wanted me to be. My aunt-mother never asked me anything about what had been done to me. She never referred to the days I was away. I felt bad that she behaved as if nothing had happened. But of course she did not forget to remind me that if I ever slept with boys, I'd lose my virginity. I was happy when school resumed and I could go back to my school friends.

"I lived with my aunt-mother until I was in Primary Five in Mweyale Primary School. Before I completed that year, my aunt-mother passed away. No one told me what had killed her. One day I simply returned from school to find mourners at home. All my brothers were older, so I was the youngest child in the home. Everybody sympathised with me, and my uncle-father was especially sad about me. Most of my brothers were away, either at boarding school or looking for jobs. So most of the time, I was alone with my uncle-father.

"That same year, 2004, I was at home one day when a strange woman came to our house. I wondered who she was, but I noticed that my uncle-father was very happy to see her. They sat and talked for a long time. I did not know what they were talking about, and I did not care, anyway. When it was time for this woman to go back to wherever she had come from, my uncle called me aside and told me to pack my clothes. At my age I had only a few clothes and nothing else.

"'You are going with her,' he told me.

"'What do you mean, going with her, Father?'

"'You are going to live with her.'

"'To live with her?'

"'Yes, my dear daughter.'

"'But who is she?'

"'You are going to live with your people. She is your mother,' he said, not quite looking at me. 'You are going home, my child.'

"'Father…' But my questions had run out. I honestly wondered why he was sending me away with a strange woman. If it were today, the days of child trafficking and child sacrifice, I would have thought that she was going to sell me as a slave or to be sacrificed.

"'I am taking you home, my daughter. I am your mother,' the strange woman said.

"When most people talk about shock, they have no idea what it means to be shocked. I was so shocked I could not believe what I was being told. Then my uncle-father and the woman talked to me for some time, and indeed I realised that my father was not my father, my mother was not my mother, and my brothers were not my brothers.

"My feeling then was, and still is, that I had been duped all my life. Although I was still in Primary Five, I was already a big girl. I had started school late and sometimes missed exams and therefore didn't always get promoted to the next class. I was mostly a domestic worker in my home. My aunt did not think that my education was a priority. I also suspect that my family's pastoralist migration played a role in my slow schooling.

"As I tried to figure out the saga of family and belonging, I remembered an incident when I had felt that my aunt-mother was a cruel mother. I thought that, as a mother, she did not have a heart big enough for me as her daughter, especially her only daughter, as I thought I was. I had accidentally burned my leg and foot. The burns were quite severe and painful. I cried so much and desperately needed both her help and her concern. I was shocked when she simply shrugged and said that I had caused the burns myself and so should suffer the consequences. She totally ignored me.

"For several days she left me on my own and did not take me for any medical attention. I was very hurt, and I spent many days hiding and crying. I was in so much pain and felt so alone. Only when the wound got infected and started to smell, and pus was running out of it, did she take me to hospital.

"As I thought about who I really was, I connected the burns incident to the time the woman I had called mother had led me to the women who made me bleed so much. I am naturally a reserved person, so I never showed her what I felt or the anger I carried in my heart towards her. I thought she was my mother and that I had no other mother. I felt very unfortunate that I had a mother like her. On the other hand, I had an excellent relationship with my brothers.

They liked me a lot and they treated me as if I were a princess living among them.

"To discover that I had another family was shocking beyond measure and raised many questions that I dared not ask anyone. My uncle-father told me that he loved me very much but that he could not continue to raise a girl on his own.

"When I asked my mother why she had never come to check on me, she told me that it was done on purpose to cut off the family ties and help me fit well into the new family. It was ironic that I now needed these ties restored to connect me to my original family.

"When I finally agreed to go with my mother, it was not because I was convinced or excited about finding my family but because my uncle-father could not keep me. I had no choice."

****

"Life in Ethiopia was not auspicious for me. My sisters and brothers had no dreams beyond grazing cows. And so I joined the gang and never went back to school. My parents' life was pastoralist – looking after cows and migrating to find pasture. They had relocated to another area, away from Mega town, where we were born, but they kept their house and land there. By 2007, I had become very restless leading a pastoralist life, and I was sure the next thing everybody was thinking about was finding me a husband. Already, a few sons of other pastoralists had started frequenting our home after my arrival. I did not want to marry any of them. I asked my parents to let me go and live in Mega town. While in Mweyale I had learned to cook well. I therefore decided that I could start a restaurant in Mega, in my parents' old house. My parents granted me permission and even gave me two cows for milk.

"I moved to Mega in March 2007 and set up Hanifa's Restaurant. People liked my food, and my business boomed. I could make very tasty naan that men came looking for all the time.

"Four months later, I was at the restaurant one day when government soldiers entered without warning and accused me of hiding rebels. At first I took it for a joke. I had no idea at all about the whereabouts of any rebels. And I thought that it should be obvious to them that I, Hanifa, would not have anything to do with rebels. Of course I had heard about the Oromo Liberation Front rebels, but all

I knew was that they existed. Where they were was not any concern of mine.

"'Show us where they are,' the soldier insisted. I could see their anger rise with each word they uttered. I told them they could search the whole house.

"'You house them! You hide them! You feed them in this restaurant,' they shouted.

"I was in shock.

"'Where is your family? Why do you live alone here? See, your family is away helping rebels.' I knew that all that my family was interested in was their cows and pasture and I, my restaurant. I denied all their accusations, but before I knew it, the soldiers were shooting in the air and at people. Everybody ran in disarray, but within seconds two bodies lay on the floor in pools of blood. The blood motif was becoming very much part of my life, and that made me so sad. I was arrested with a few other people who did not manage to escape.

"The soldiers took us to their camp, where they imprisoned us in small, dark rooms. I was locked up in my own room, and for three days I did not see anyone. On the fourth day, they let me out in the evening and gave me a heap of their clothes to wash. After the washing, they took me back inside, and I felt slightly relieved that I had seen the outside. I was drifting into sleep when I heard the door open again. It was dark, and I did not see who was entering, but I could tell there were three or four people.

"I waited for them to speak, but talk was not what had brought them. Without saying a word, they descended on me. One pinned my arms to the ground while another held my legs apart. The third raped me. He entered me again and again, and every time it felt like a sharp knife cutting right through my heart and into my brain. There were quick shuffles, and then another was on top of me, and then another, until I lay still and closed my mind to who I was or what was happening. Every time I remember that experience, I get a splitting headache."

For the first time during Hanifa's narrative, she breaks into sobs that reflect both mental anguish and the memory of physical pain. We offer her a glass of water, but she does not take it. She rubs her temples and stares into space. Tears freely cascade down the valleys and ridges of her young but weather-beaten face.

As she describes the desecration, it weighs heavily on us too as we listen. Her story becomes our story. A story of womanhood violated. Our hearts reach out to her, and we grieve together. Not even our lecture on the interviewer's duty of impartiality can hold back our tears or take away the lumps in our throats.

"From that day on, soldiers would enter my room and rape me repeatedly. It was not possible to tell who was who. It was the most painful experience of my life, even worse than the 'circumcision' I had gone through. Every night, three-four-five soldiers desecrated my body. I could only tell when it was not the same man by the different sizes that tore into me. Every night was a nightmare. That was when I came to understand the essence of women's 'circumcision', because as the men raped me repeatedly, they talked.

"'This girl is a miracle come to us. The secret behind her tightness is beyond what we have ever experienced in this camp. She opens for us every night and closes after we leave. Every night we are eating a virgin, the secret of 'circumcision',' they would say, and laugh in a very vulgar manner.

"That was when I understood that I was different. That I was not like other women. That it was no longer a case of virginity but a war on my womanhood."

That was the point where Hanifa understood the virginity she had received from the women in Mweyale. The women had taken away the essence of her womanhood and turned her into a sexual object.

"The soldiers would tear into me every night. Every encounter was a new opening, a new breaking of virginity, their new pleasure, my new pangs of pain. Every night I begged these men to kill me. I begged them not to leave me alive, but they laughed at me, their voices resounding against the dark room as they left me for dead. Sometimes I passed out and woke up hours later with pain that only I could understand.

"A few days after the rapes started, intense itching began in my genitals. From then on, every time they entered me, I would get a sharp pain as if they were thrusting very sharp nails deep into my uterus. It was painful, very, very painful. The pain almost drove me insane. After the soldiers left the room, the pain would persist all night long and throughout the next day. I could not sleep, could not sit, and could not stand. I would spend the whole night shifting, trying to find a less painful position. I would squat one minute, kneel down the next, thinking I was going to die. The beasts who raped me did not care about my pain. Every evening they fetched me from the lockup and told me either to cook for them or to wash their clothes. I would limp around and do the work. I did not need to know which of them had been in my lockup during the night. I hated them all, with a passion!"

We wondered why Hanifa had to do the soldiers' laundry in the evenings. She said that the timing was intentional. They did not take prisoners out during the day because they did not want those passing by the camp to see them and report to their relatives. Evening was better, when they were less likely to be seen. The soldiers wanted the prisoners to die in prison without ever being discovered.

As Hanifa tells her story, one feels that hate is too mild a word for her emotion. It is not enough just to hate the soldiers. Surely there must be a stronger word. Something beyond hate, something beyond disgust, something beyond the evil in the human heart that would match their beastly actions.

"When a war is out in the open, it is easy to know what is going on and to get help from the outside world. The war in Ethiopia is silent and deadly. The world will never know exactly what goes on there," Hanifa reflects gloomily.

"On 10 August in 2007, a fight broke out in the camp. I don't even know who was fighting whom, but there was a lot of commotion involving soldiers. That evening, I was outside with an old man. I don't quite remember what he was doing. When the soldiers who were guarding us ran in the direction of the fight, the old man quickly walked over to me and told me to run away. 'Pick clothes from that heap and put them on. No one will notice. They are too busy now trying to save their own skin. Just run. By the time they come looking for you, you will be out of sight. I will do whatever I can to divert their attention.'

"'Let's go together, father, let's escape together,' I said.

"'No, I am old and wasted. I will stay. But you, my daughter, you have your whole life before you. Let's not waste time. Go!' He showed me the direction to take.

"'Don't look back. Just keep walking, my daughter. If they are to kill you, let them do so while you are on the road to your freedom.'

"Quickly I picked up a jacket from the heap of clothes and limped away. There were no goodbyes, and I was soon out of the camp. I was surprised to find other people running away, and I joined them. We ran for a long distance and then saw a truck and stopped it. The driver told us that he was heading for Mweyale. The mention of Mweyale, my former home, made me feel as if I were already there. I was so excited when he agreed to take us on top of his truck. He told us to lie flat and not to raise our heads. We jumped onto his truck, and he drove off.

"When he finally stopped and called us to disembark, we were in Mweyale-Ethiopia, on the border with Mweyale-Kenya, where I had spent my childhood. I jumped off the truck, leaving the stolen jacket there. I then walked ahead smartly, greeting a few people I recognised in that part of town. I behaved as if I had not been gone for years, as if I had just crossed the border to buy a needle or bread at the Mweyale-Ethiopia border. This was something we often did when I lived in Mweyale-Kenya, and I knew a number of people in the shops and the tricks of crossing to and fro.

"I don't know where the other people on the truck went, but I mingled with the locals and walked straight home. I was delighted to find my uncle-father there. For the three years I had been away, I had never been in contact with him. I think our people are strange. We just keep away from one another without feeling guilty. But of course the conditions do not favour constant communication.

"When I told him my story, his face turned cloudy. 'They will follow you here,' he said. 'Those people are very dangerous.' He told me how they had been following people and killing them in Mweyale and other surrounding villages. 'No, my daughter, you can't stay here.'

"'But where can I go?'

"'Somewhere far from here, go to Uganda.'

"'How do I go to Uganda?'

"'You have no choice, my daughter.'

"'Please, Father, let me stay.'

"'No, I am sorry. When you get to Uganda, ask for any Ethiopian or Somali, and they will help you. There are many Ethiopians and Somalis in Uganda.'

"My life had become a life of no choice indeed. Uncle-father gave me some money, and I travelled with his friend to Nairobi on a fuel tanker. It was a very long journey, and for some reason it took longer than necessary. Along the way the driver left me on the tanker and went away, to his home, which I later learnt was Masabiti village. He was away for about five days, and I stayed on the tanker alone. But his people brought me food every day.

"We later moved on to Nairobi, and I was directed to Akamba Bus Station, where I got a bus to Uganda. That was a very long journey too. I used all the money my uncle had given me to pay for the bus ticket. I did not have any money left. By the time I arrived in Kampala, I was hungry, I was spent, and I knew no one in Uganda. But I had one wish – to survive it all.

"I did not get off the bus in a hurry. I waited for everyone to disembark, then I followed. I had been warned that people might take advantage of me if they noticed I was a stranger. So I took a bit of time and located the friendly young face of a woman seated on a bench at the station."

On this note, Hanifa's face brightens. She looks at us as if we should know what happened next.

"Aha?" We quickly prompt her.

"This girl had Ethiopian neighbours. Can you imagine? I felt as if she had said that my family lived just across the road and all I had to do was walk over and say, 'Hello there!' The girl took me to her neighbours straightaway. I later learned that was Nsambya village and that the Good Samaritan was called Juliet.

"It was a family of Ethiopian girls. And they lived with their mother in the same compound but in different houses."

Hanifa's face takes on another twist. The cloud returns, and she rubs her temples again. We feel her pain again, the pain that comes with the memory of rape in the Ethiopian camp.

"The girls welcomed me very warmly and gave me a room to share with them. They were very friendly. I was a bit surprised when they told me that I could join them in their business, so that together we could make some money to survive on. I was happy and agreed to join them. They said that I would like the business and that it was lucrative. They did not even wait for me to settle in before they asked me to join them. When they finally brought me clothes and told me to dress so we could go out for business, I was taken aback. Their business was prostitution on Kampala streets! I was not ready for anything that involved sex, and I told them so.

"'How do you think you will survive?' They tortured me with endless rude questions. How could I tell them that I was not like them?

I just told them that I was not able to join them, and I begged them to let me be their housemaid instead. Finally one day they tormented me too much, and I decided that enough was enough. As they dressed to go out for business, I went out and returned with a packet of quinine tablets from a drug shop. I had heard that quinine could kill you if you took an overdose of it.

"As soon as they left the house, I swallowed all the tablets and went to bed. I wanted to die in bed. I was very sure that this was the end of the road for me. I was tired of trying to run away from myself. For hours I waited for the tablets to work and start me sweating. I expected to start vomiting and dying. Instead, I drifted into a sweet, deep slumber unlike anything I had experienced for weeks. I woke up the next morning feeling completely fresh, as if I had taken a sedative or painkiller. That was when I decided I was going to live and live.

"The following day, I asked Juliet to help me. She took me to Old Kampala Police Station, where I started the process of registration as a refugee.

"In my journey to gain refugee status, I met people who came to change my life. I met a refugee woman operating a small restaurant in Kisenyi. Because I had experience in restaurants, I asked her for a job. When she agreed, I also started a side business of making mandazi and chapatti. Customers would ask for them, but she did not have them. I left the girls in Nsambya, and the restaurant became my new home. I would wait for all the customers to leave in the evening, then I would make my bed there and sleep.

"While I was working at the restaurant, a middle-aged man became very interested in my mandazi. He ate them for breakfast and for supper, but in the end it was clear that it was not the mandazi but the mandazi-maker who interested him. I liked him too, and we talked quite a lot whenever the restaurant was not very busy. Eventually he proposed marriage. Much as I liked him, when he proposed, my heart sank. I had enjoyed our chats, and I had even flirted with him a little, but that is where I wanted our relationship to end. I knew I would never want to have another sexual encounter.

"One day when he insisted on the issue, I plucked up the courage to tell him about my body and my sexual experiences. I told him that I was not a woman like other women. He was sympathetic and convinced me that it must have been because of rape that sex had hurt. He promised to help me out if I accepted him.

"It took me time to decide, but when I finally accepted him, I experienced the same pain all over again. Gentle as he was with me, he still tore into me, and I still felt the sharp pains, even long after the sexual act. He apologised and said he was going to ensure that I got help somehow. A few weeks after our marriage blessing at the mosque, I was granted full refugee status. I was forced to go to Nakivale Refugee Camp. Though we had already been to the mosque and were already husband and wife, the law did not recognise our marriage. And so I left my husband. But we remained in touch, via the telephone especially, and sometimes he came to the camp to visit me.

"Camp life is very interesting. The government just packs you off to a camp. You don't know anyone there, there is no house for you, there is no one to receive you, there is no system for newcomers to follow, and no one tells you what to do upon arrival. But when I got there, I was fortunate to quickly find an Ethiopian family of the Oromo Borana tribe like me. It was a very loving family, and I lived with them. Unfortunately, the results of my rape in the Ethiopian prison and of my 'circumcision' in Mweyale had followed me across borders. The itching in my genitals had now become intense. Off and on, I continued to get attacks of sharp pain tearing into my lower abdomen.

"One day I decided to go to the health centre at the camp. While I was waiting to see the doctor, a mother walked in carrying a small girl whose dress was soaked in blood. Blood again! The mother and daughter went straight into the examining room. Within a few minutes, everyone at the hospital was whispering about the girl. She was eight years old, and she had just been sexually molested by a thirty-year-old man. People were describing the girl, and everybody who had seen her would know who she was. I felt angry at them all and thought that they were being unfair to the little girl. Telling everyone what had happened to her was very wrong. And mind you, no one was describing the man who had hurt her. It was the innocent girl who was now being stigmatised.

"When I saw all that, I knew that if I entered the doctor's examination room, by the time I came out, everyone at the camp would know what my problems were. I had intended to tell the doctor everything and even to show him my scars in order for him to give me the best help. What happened to the little girl made me change my mind, and I carried my troubles back to my Borana family.

"I called my husband and told him about my pains. He advised me to get a letter allowing me to leave the camp and go for treatment in Kampala. With his advice, I eventually contacted people at the Refugee Law Project who connected me to the African Centre for the Treatment of Torture Victims. At ACTV, I was counselled, and for the first time in years I got proper medical attention. The ACTV doctors referred me to Bugolobi Nursing Home, where I underwent a three-hour corrective surgery on my private parts. Through it all, my husband was there for me. It took about one month for me to heal from the surgical wounds. That was towards the end of 2008.

"The wicked circumcisers had sealed me off. They had left only a little opening. After the operation, I was surprised when I could hear the sound of my urine being passed. Before, urine had had to be squeezed out drop by drop. During menstruation, I had had to push out clots as if birthing a baby. My menstrual cramps were always excruciating. To be honest, I cannot understand why a normal, straight-thinking person would subject his daughter to such ugly and unbearable pain. I feel sad for Somali women and women from Ethiopian tribes that circumcise, and for other women of the world who undergo 'circumcision'.

"At the same time, I am conscious of my linkages to the Somali people. If by any chance I ever had daughters, I would protect and defend them against this dehumanising custom. Even from my grave, my spirit would still protect my children, their children, and the children of their children. I ask Allah to grant my spirit that power! Unfortunately, since the prison rapes, I have never had any menstrual periods. The doctors say that I contracted a sexually transmitted infection that, coupled with the rape damage, may have affected my reproductive system. I am grateful for one thing, that maybe if this had not happened, those scoundrels would have made me pregnant. What would I have told their offspring?"

Hanifa is visibly angry, and we empathise with her. It is indeed God's providence that she did not get pregnant at the time.

"Recently I was shown a Somali woman in Kisenyi, Kampala, who circumcises Somali girls in Uganda. I went to her and confronted her. I told her that I was going to report her to the police if she continued to cut girls. She then said that if I dared to do so, she would make me walk naked on the streets. Maybe she feels that she has special powers, but I know she does not. People like her only create fear in society. If I saw her cutting any girl, I would attack her. Even if I were killed in the process, I would rescue the girl.

"I would like the government of Uganda and the concerned women working in NGOs to know that 'circumcision' is going on right under their noses in the Somali refugee communities. These girls need help. Some may need to be operated on and reconstructed as I was, while others need to be protected from the cutting before it happens. And because of the assumption that the girls are still virgins at the time of 'circumcision', the circumcisers do not take precautions against HIV transmission during the ritual. I strongly believe that the razor blade that cut me was the same one used to cut the other girls with whom I was circumcised."

We make a silent promise to fight for the girls. We promise to distribute Hanifa's story to as many girls as possible. Then we ask her what she thinks of her future. She brightens up and smiles.

"After the operation I now feel like a woman. I enjoy sex with my husband. Of course, sometimes I am apprehensive about it, especially in the dark. But at least when he touches me these days, my blood warms in anticipation. Before the operation I was like a piece of wood. Now I want to have children of my own. Before, I was afraid that if I dared to get pregnant I would die in labour. So many circumcised women die during childbirth. But my husband has taught me to trust again. I think he is a loving man, and he is playing a big role in my reconstruction. He tells me that sometimes I scream in the night and also talk a lot in my sleep, but I believe all that will go away with time."

We are surprised that Hanifa speaks very good English. One cannot believe that she is a Primary Five dropout.

"I am still interested in cooking, and maybe I will set up another Hanifa's Restaurant in the future. I have had to do a lot of self-education, and I watch TV, looking at some programmes where I can learn a few things.

"I have no idea how my family in Ethiopia is. But I do not really miss them. I instead miss Mweyale, I miss my brothers and my uncle-father. Maybe someday I will look them up. But a refugee's life is a prison of its own. My prayer for Ethiopia is that she heals from wounds of war so that we can return home someday. Unfortunately, the wounds are festering from underneath. But for now, life has to continue, and I am a part of it."

Life has to continue indeed, but which direction is it taking for the girls whose womanhood is being violated by traditional systems in their communities? This is a battle we should all fight. It is not just Hanifa's battle. It is our battle too to fight FGM. The world needs whole women. When petals of a flower are blown away in the wind, the flower is no longer a flower but something else.

Tezira Jamwa

The Ungodly Scalpel

Oh you the ungodly scalpel!
How merciless you can be
How dare you invade my innocence
My privacy!
You make my innocence the theatre of onlookers
Chanting with insatiable pleasure
Wanting to witness my transformation into adulthood
How degrading!
But the ancestors have spoken

Oh you the ungodly scalpel!
How violent you can be
Rendering me helpless and powerless
The old witch with scarlet eyes wielding your unhygienic body
with glee
Ready for the abominable act
The moment has come
Yanking my two helpless limbs apart
It is done!
Challenging the anatomy

Oh you the ungodly scalpel!
You ride on the rhythm of oppressive culture
How can I escape the treachery
The crude and unhealthy action
Leaves me in untold pain
How dare you torture my youthful body
What type of inequality is this?
Where is my physical integrity?
You control my sexuality

Oh you the ungodly scalpel!
Tweaking away at the centre of pleasure
You are inhuman
I hate you for your cruelty
My monthly visitation is a nightmare
The bleeding, the shock and the trauma I live for life make me
crazy
Honestly, is this the right path to prepare me for adulthood?
By making my person ugly and riddled with grizzly spots
Surely this is a violation of my human rights and freedom

Oh you the ungodly scalpel!
You make procreation a nightmare
The agony, the gnashing of teeth torment me
The tortuous ripples make me unconscious
I have no feelings for the great moment
You make Romeo and Juliet appear unromantic
Why?
Because you have robbed my treasure and innocence

Oh you the ungodly scalpel!
Where can I go, where can I hide myself?
Even when I fly abroad, you still follow me
To perform the abominable act
Three million of us worldwide every year succumb to your desire
Who will come to our rescue
Is it the custodians of culture themselves
The women?

Oh you the ungodly scalpel!
You are a cold-blooded barbarian!

Linda Lillian

The Unwilling Sacrificial Lamb

Not my choice
Not by chance
All these gifts they bring
To deceive me
Will not blur the anguish
That makes the scene

Excited old women
Telling of the glory of 'circumcision'
The bravery of young women
Led to the altar of womanhood
Like lambs for sacrifice
Told not to screech or shudder
To be women

I am already a woman
Glorified by the nature of my make
What is this sacrifice
Where I am the sacrifice
Sacrificing a bit of me
For the glory of one day ritual
That seals my fate permanently?

Lillian Tindyebwa

Beyond the Music and the Dance

I could hardly believe her when she told me her age. She was born in 1948 in Kisenyi village, in the then-Sebei District, in the part now renamed Kapchorwa. At sixty, she looked almost ten years younger, with self-confidence and a lively demeanour.

Grace was of medium height with an oval face and a smooth, chocolate-brown complexion. This was my fifth day in Kapchorwa, and I had noticed that people of this area smiled a lot, and their very white teeth made their smiles magnificent. This woman was no different, and her smile helped me relax and look forward to our interview.

"Habari (How are you)?" I greeted her in Kiswahili as we sat together waiting for the interpreter.

"Muzuri (Fine)," she replied. I was happy to make this little opening and to be able to communicate with her directly. I did not want this chance to pass.

"Pole, ume ngojea sana (Sorry you had to wait so long)," I continued, praying that her Kiswahili was good enough to allow us to proceed with the conversation. I knew that many Ugandans did not speak it well, but at least people in the eastern part of Uganda know a bit of Kiswahili, since they are close to Kenya.

"Hakuna tabu (It is okay)," she answered with a smile. We were doing quite well, I thought, and then the interpreter arrived.

****

The month of November is usually a dry season in Kapchorwa, but this year it was wet and cold. The weather was similar to that of southern Uganda, where the wet November season brings grasshoppers out of their hiding places only to be caught and turned into a mouthwatering delicacy. The month of November is in fact called musenene in most of the Bantu languages, meaning "the month of grasshoppers." Women are now allowed to eat the crispy winged treat, which was once reserved for men only.

As I interacted more with the Sabiny, especially the women that I interviewed, I realised that the inhabitants of this highland region, with all its seemingly undisturbed beauty, still held concepts and beliefs unchanged since their ancestors had brought them from ancient Egypt under the Pharaoh -- who, fearing that his numerous women might get amorous with his servants, decided to mutilate their genitals to reduce their sexual desire.

I heard from these friendly people that during the time a Sabiny girl is growing up, one of the things that she is told, apart from the requirement of 'circumcision', is that, even if she studies to the highest level, she will have to come back to her home area, to live, get married, and work there all her life. Sabiny girls grow up knowing these things, learnt by heart during the time of innocence when children take in all that they hear from the grown-ups as the truth, the whole truth, and nothing but the truth.

The journey to this mountainside town had been hot until we started ascending the lush, steep slopes. As we climbed, I remembered the words of that long-ago colonial master, Winston Churchill, who on his visit to the British colonies in 1903 described Uganda as "the Pearl of Africa." Churchill talked of climbing up, as in the story of "Jack and the Bean Stalk," to reach the heights of Uganda. I wondered whether he could have had Kapchorwa in mind. Going up these slopes, pristine and mysterious, was indeed breath-taking.

Kapchorwa town sits at the top of a plateau shaped like a giant altar cup held up by a hidden rocky hand. You drive up and seem to go up and up without seeing the end of the road, past the magnificent Sipi Falls, then levelling off to the plateau upon which the town perches. Nature seems to have left just enough space for the town before resuming the ascent to Mt. Elgon's higher reaches.

Although the journey had been long, tiring, and almost endless, the people in our shared minibus had made it pleasant by their friendly manner. They all spoke the same language, and they talked as if they were very familiar with one another. Kapchorwa is indeed a small town, and they probably did know each other. At first, my colleague and I stood out as strangers, but we soon found that the Sabiny people were amiable, and conversation flowed from one end of the minibus to the other.

An organisation called REACH offers hope to the women of this remote place. At their offices I met and talked with Grace.

I had already read everything I could lay my hands on to understand what FGM was all about. Was it as destructive and dangerous as we all believed it to be? If so, what kind of parents would allow their little girl to undergo such a brutal and unnecessary practice? I listened with deep interest as Grace told her story.

"I grew up surrounded by a loving family. Like any other child, I looked forward to the day when I would have my own family," she began.

"I later discovered, however, that my father loved us, his daughters, particularly because he viewed us as a source of wealth. He looked forward to the time when men would come to marry us and pay him the bride price.

"Our family consisted of six girls. He could reap a lot of bride wealth from such a number. We had one brother living in this gold mine of girls. The two men in the family must have inwardly been thanking their lucky stars for the treasure that we were. But at the time, the fact that we girls were primarily viewed as a source of wealth did not bother us. Indeed, even today, many women simply accept it as a fact of life.

"My mother, however, silently wanted me, above everything else, to study. So she arranged for me to go to Kenya, where her brother lived. The Sabiny are ethnically related to the Kalenjins of Kenya, and many of us have relatives across the border. My family was no different.

"That was how I was able to stay in Kenya for most of my primary school education. Kenya was a good place, and I liked living with my cousins. But after Primary Six I was sent home, believing that I was coming only for a visit and would be going back to continue my education.

"Until now I have never been able to establish whether my uncle had a plan when he sent me home at that particular time or if it was just a stroke of bad timing that changed my life forever. Later on in life, when I thought back, I suspected that my uncle could have thought I had reached the age for initiation and chose to send me home during the 'circumcision' season. As you know, among the Sabiny 'circumcision' is done during the month of December in every even-numbered year, though preparations for it start much earlier. In the months preceding the ceremonies, there is a lot of dancing and singing and drinking of the local brew. The dancing actually starts in August and goes on till December.

"When I came home, I found a number of my friends were about to be circumcised. I was not so keen on going through this ritual, and I was not under any pressure to do so. So I kept my distance, but not for long. My friends persuaded me to join them. They described the dances. They demonstrated all the moves that they could make with their young bodies to the sound of drums and singing. They told me about the gifts they had received, and I made up my mind to join them. But I have lived to regret my decision." Grace sounded very sad as she recounted her tale.

"I started taking part in the dances, at first not seriously. I remember it all. I really believed it was all a harmless pastime and I would get out of it at the right time.

"There are things I did not know. I discovered too late that when one joins the 'circumcision' candidates, she surrenders her personal free will and becomes part of the crowd. One has to do what everyone else is doing. The young girls dance in groups from house to house in the villages, receiving presents as encouragement, including kitenge wrappers, chickens, and even goats. It seems to be the time of one's life! That is how I missed the right moment to leave. With all the excitement, the temptation always to stay a little longer was almost magnetic. It's funny, but even as the days sped by I kept thinking that I would leave the ceremonies soon -- but soon never came. You see, as they dance, the women sing songs of courage and bravery. They sound the drums, and everyone gets lost in it all. It is such infectious fun. For the young, it is totally irresistible.

"One thing I remember, though, is that whenever the drumming and the dancing stopped, I felt different. And for a long time I remained uncertain about the whole thing. Deep inside my heart I believed I would never go through with it. My parents were not pushing me at all, which was not the case with some other families. It was entirely up to me to make up my mind. At various moments I felt a tug of war inside me – should I go ahead with 'circumcision' or should I not? Meanwhile I continued with the nightly dances, getting lost in the beautiful sounds of the tam-tam, accompanied by the voices of the girls singing odes to the glory of becoming a real woman.

"Probably I would have withdrawn from it all if something had not been introduced to lead me further on, beyond the music and the dance. You see, among the Sabiny, traditional medicines are used for many purposes, and they are especially common in the 'circumcision' rituals. One specific medicine is meant to increase a girl's boldness just before she undergoes the cutting. It is used to uplift one's mood and dispel any doubts. After taking the medicine, one feels a sudden upsurge of courage and readiness to face the knife. The feeling is so overwhelming that a former coward will start demanding that the surgeon come immediately. This medicine is administered so easily -- it is just inhaled.

"I had a friend called Chelimo, who believed so much in the practice. Together with the mentor, she persuaded me. I remember the conversation because I used to think about it a lot.

"'Just inhale a little,' the mentor said, but I was hesitant.

"'Do not be left out! You don't want to remain a child, do you?' Chelimo asked.

"'Chelimo is right,' added the mentor, 'everyone will be a woman except you.'

"They followed me around for two days, talking about nothing else but that. Eventually I agreed to sniff the medicine. But even as I started to take it, I wasn't sure. I decided I would breathe in just a little, but Chelimo and the mentor were there to urge me on and ensure that the whole dose was taken. And as soon as I inhaled it, I felt dizzy, as if I had taken a strong drug, and I told them I wanted to rest. They said it was all right, and I lay down outside, under a tree. I woke after about an hour feeling fine, and all my fears were gone. I felt so bold, but I have lived to regret it," Grace added, gazing blankly across the room.

"The night before the 'circumcision', I was one of those girls who danced most and sang loudest. We sang songs of courage that had been sung by our ancestors long before us. The words seemed loaded with a new meaning, and I suddenly found great pleasure in sharing them with friends and age-mates, lost in the rhythm of song and dance. I was very happy as I jumped to the frenzied sound of the drums. It felt good to know that these songs were the same ones our great-grandmothers had sung. It was inspiring. We felt close to our Sabiny ancestors, and I believed that since it was something they approved and practised, then 'circumcision' had to be good.

"The merrymaking went on throughout the night. My father and mother and many other relatives were there. They had brewed plenty of beer and had slaughtered animals, and that made the feast big and exciting. I felt happy and proud to be the reason they were all gathered there that night. We danced the whole night, and those who shared the local brew had an unforgettable time.

"Since I had not slept, there was no question of waking up at dawn. The mentor had done her job of taking us through the 'training' of the previous night. I had listened with awe to the secrets passed on from generation to generation, secrets that I can never reveal to an uncircumcised person."

"What about now?" I asked. "Surely you know that nothing will happen to you if you tell me," I said. "Just tell me a few carefully selected and interesting points."

"You see, my sister," Grace began after a brief silence. My heart was racing. I thought that I was about to have the privilege of learning the secrets of the Sabiny. But I was disappointed.

All she said was, "I made a vow, my sister, and I cannot break it."

I was surprised that after so many years, and after all that she had gone through as a result of her 'circumcision', this woman still adhered to her oath never to spill the Sabiny beans.

"I will tell you about the 'circumcision' but not about the Sabiny secrets, that's all," she said with a smile. I was reminded of the Mafia we used to read about during our school days, and their oath of silence known as omertà. This was a kind of omertà – I had no doubt about this in my mind.

"On the day we were circumcised, just before dawn, we had to go and bathe in the river under the supervision of the mentor. It was not just a normal bath at the river. There were rituals there too, which I cannot talk about. After the rituals at the river, we eventually went back to my father's compound, where we were made to stand in a line. I was among the first ones to be cut. I felt no fear. I was ready to go through it all."

At this point, Grace grew silent. I did not press her to continue, but at the same time I wanted to hear it all.

Then she resumed. "The circumciser worked very fast, and soon it was my turn. I had watched my cousin, who had stood just in front of me, and she had not shown any emotion as the knife touched her body. I had to follow her example.

"When the knife touched me that cold December morning, I groaned deep in my throat -- oh, oh, oh! The pain was unimaginable. I had never felt so much pain before. I thought I was going to faint, but the mentor had clearly instructed us. There was to be no screaming or twisting of the body. So I bit my lips and closed my eyes. They had told us that if we did not stay still, or if we tried to run or scream, they would call the 'muscle men' to hold us as we were being cut. I knew it was not a mere threat -- they could do it. Nobody wanted men staring at them at such a point of weakness, so I had to endure the pain.

"'Go now,' said the circumciser. I heard her voice, but it seemed to be coming from far away. The sound was loud and full of echoes. I got up and started walking to the house where the others were. My groin seemed to be on fire. The pain was unbearable, and I cried silently. Remember, there was no painkiller, not even a local herb. Each one of us had to stand up and walk back to the house on her own. I was dazed, and I have never been able to understand how I made it to the house.

"Later, I heard the voice of the mentor as she came to check my wound. I did not want anybody to make me open my legs, but I had no choice. As she looked at me, she commented that my wound was bleeding a lot, more than the others'. At times the circumciser accidentally leaves part of what is meant to be excised, and it is the work of the mentor to check and ensure that the genitals are completely gone. Even when the mentor comes to check on the girls, she uses a knife to do so. She actually scrapes at the drying part of the wound to see how it is healing. Luckily, all that they wanted to remove in my case had been cut away so there was no question of doing anything more. It was a relief to me because I did not think I could really go through more cutting."

I asked Grace why she had not been taken to hospital after they realised that she was bleeding a lot.

"My sister, we lived up there in the forest. There was no hospital. People there did not believe in rushing others to hospital," she said between clenched teeth. The tone of hopelessness was unmistakable. When I looked at her I saw that her face was now grim and withdrawn.

"My recovery was slow. The bleeding from the wound lasted more than a month. I tell you, my sister, it was terrible. I cannot find stronger words to describe my situation. I was in so much pain, and it was no longer just the wound that hurt but it was as if every part of me resonated with the pain. I felt so afraid because I thought I would die. The endless bleeding was hard to bear. And all the time I remembered that I had not wanted to go through this 'circumcision'. So over and above the physical pain, I blamed myself. I was consumed with regret.

"During this time, the only medicine available to us was our own urine. You see, each circumcised girl is told that there is no medicine apart from their urine, and that to make it work, they have to press their legs together while they urinate. This causes the warm liquid to enter the wound and help it to heal. The urine stings and burns, and the girl must overcome her fear to force the urine onto the wound. So what we did, and I know it is still done even today, was to hold onto a tree trunk, wrap our arms around it in a tight embrace, cross our legs, and pass the urine. Holding on to the tree helped us to go through the excruciating pain without screaming. If a girl was afraid to urinate because of the pain, the mentors would beat her. I was very worried about the whole experience. I lost a lot of weight. I would cry all night long because of my pain and fear.

"One morning when I woke up, I did not feel the usual wetness. But I dared not even open my legs and just stayed where I lay in the room, waiting for the mentor, who was still coming to check on me daily. This time she announced that the wound was no longer bleeding.

"I was so relieved and happy to see the end of that ordeal, but much later I was to discover that all that bleeding had represented irreparable damage. My menstrual periods no longer came regularly, as they had before the 'circumcision', and when they did they were very painful. But there was nothing I could do. As I told you, there was no hospital nearby, and it was not our culture to rush to hospitals anyway.

"In this place there was nobody to whom I could tell my problem and hope to get assistance. I don't remember ever visiting a doctor as I was growing up. I just had to bear it all as I had been taught, as a brave woman. I lived with it all. As soon as I had recovered from the initial pain and bleeding, I enrolled in the local school near home. My dream was to be a teacher. Unfortunately, I never got anywhere near becoming a teacher. One thing you have to understand about our culture: 'circumcision' is a rite of passage to womanhood, and it seems to be a way of declaring to the world that a woman is ready for marriage, whether she is in school or not. So, if according to culture I was ready for marriage, then that was it. I could not run away or appeal to anybody to protect me.

"One day, about six months after my 'circumcision', as I was walking from school with some friends, I noticed a group of young men walking behind us, apparently going in the same direction. I did not feel particularly worried about them because it was broad daylight and I was not walking alone. There were many other school girls and boys at different points along the road.

"Two of the young men passed by us and then suddenly stopped about ten metres ahead. Then they came back, as if they had forgotten something. Meanwhile, two others were coming from behind. Although now I felt a little uneasy, I did not think that I was a target until one of them came and stood in front of me, blocking my way. I told him to get out of my way so that I could pass, but that seemed to incense him. He grabbed my hand. The others joined him, and they forced me to walk in another direction. They started beating me as we moved along the path. I was totally overcome with fear.

"After what seemed like an eternity, we reached the home of a certain old man, and the young men told me that I was to stay there and become his wife. I was crying and shaking with anger. They told me harshly to keep quiet. That was how it was in those days. Nobody could do anything, not even my parents. This was one of the accepted methods of marriage in the Kapchorwa of the 1960s. Once a girl was circumcised, she could be 'grabbed' in that manner. It was an accepted custom. Once married, I had to learn to like my husband. He was an older man who had two other wives already. I soon settled down to my new life and forgot my dream of becoming a teacher."

Grace looked like a cheerful woman, but at times sadness flickered through her eyes and reflected the pains of her life. I saw the flicker again, and at that moment I shared her pain, her loss.

"I began settling down to a new life. That was my home, and I tried to fit in as much as I could, but bedtime was not my favourite time. The scar at times causes pain when a circumcised woman tries to have sex."

I asked her why it was so when she had also told me that when a girl got circumcised, she became very marketable for marriage.

"You see, the scar is dry and hard, and it causes a lot of difficulty during sex. At first, I wondered if there was something wrong with me because I had been made to understand that it would be good when one got married. But I hardly had any sexual desire for this man, not because I did not like him -- with time we had become quite friendly – but because I felt nothing! And as for him, of course he was normal, and he expected normal relations. So we would literally fight before I gave in. Yes, our bedtime was a time for fighting over sex, because I did not have any desire for him while he found me very desirable. I was his young wife who had no feelings at all that you could remotely describe as sexual desire. I never wanted him near me in that sense, and that caused us several fights.

"I believe the men of Kapchorwa understand that female 'circumcision' affects women in that way, and to compensate they marry many women. I believe too that my husband married me because the others would no longer have sex with him every time he wanted it. Unfortunately for him, I turned out to be the same as the others.

"Soon, there was another hurdle for me. One year passed, two years, three years, four years, five full years, and there was not a sign of pregnancy. What was I to do? I wanted a baby badly. I tried some of our traditional medicines, but nothing worked. I was given all kinds of remedies, as you can imagine. And every time I tried a new one my hopes would go up, but then tumble down when my next period arrived. Like any other man, of course, my husband wanted children from me, and so he shared my frustrations and anguish, but not as desperately since he had children from his two other wives.

"At first I resented the fact that he was such an old man, but in the long run, it was an advantage for me. He was more understanding and calm, maybe because he knew he had other children already.

"When I was first desperately trying out medicines, it hurt me to imagine that he did not mind whether I gave him a child or not. But later I realised that it was better that way. Additionally, in our culture, it is normal for men to marry in old age in order to have someone to take care of them when they are old. It was clear that it was going to be my duty, rather than his older wives', to take care of our husband. They, of course, assisted me, but as the youngest wife I was assigned the responsibility.

"But, my sister, I have always known, without a shred of doubt, that my barrenness was a result of the 'circumcision'. I did not need a medical person to tell me that. I was not the only one who developed the problem. Among those who were circumcised at the same time as me, a number also failed to conceive. What happened to me was not surprising. The circumciser is not trained. She teaches herself or learns on the job, and I suspect that our particular circumciser must have cut us in a way that resulted in that permanent damage.

"Many times I have wished to turn the clock back so that I could reverse the decision I made then. It was a terrible mistake, and I have lived to regret it. I often replay in my mind the dancing and the music that attracted me to join my friends, and I remember the day I decided to inhale the medicine. But it was all the folly of youth.

"My husband died a few years ago. He was very old. But I still live in his homestead together with the other wives, without any problem. Our relationships had always been good. I believe when they saw that I could not give birth, I became less of a threat. They saw that there would be no rivalry between my children and theirs for inheritance."

I looked at Grace as she concluded her story. I thanked God in my heart that nobody was threatening to throw her out of her home, as often happens to childless women, who have no children to fight for them.

"Fortunately, I get along well with the children of my co-wives. In fact, one of them helped me when I wanted to start my crafts business. My regret in life is that the campaign against female genital mutilation started when it was already too late for me, though at the same time I am happy I have lived to see the start of programmes intended to eliminate this horrible custom. It seems to be a Sabiny tradition to use force on the body. For example, in the past they used to remove one's front teeth by force. When a person got tetanus or lockjaw, the sufferer could not open his mouth, and they said the reason for knocking out the teeth was that if one fell sick in that way they could still administer medicine. My prayer now is to see an end to tortures like these. The new generation should be protected against these practices."

As I looked at Grace's handicrafts and tried to decide which ones to buy, I was still thinking about the Sabiny and their culture.

"I will take these two," I said, settling for a miniature basket and a crescent-shaped woven utensil I liked but whose use I did not quite understand.

"How about this one?" she asked, showing me a calabash that she had cut to make it look like a cup, but with a pointed bottom that would not allow it to sit like a normal cup.

"No," I said, "let me take the two I have already chosen."

After I paid, she gave me the calabash cup as well and said, "Take this because we have now become friends."

We shook hands.

My friend Grace, I think of you and I thank you for being brave, and for your present to me, which I will always keep. The strange cup, especially, that does not balance on the table, will always remind me of Kapchorwa.

Alal Sophie Brenda

Walking on these Heavy Hills

The blades of the community
hang above me,
As if the culture steeped in them
should start falling
furiously
over my head.
As I walk on these heavy hills.

Jennifer A. Okech

I say no more!

I say no more
To the inhuman barga
Forcing its way without knocking;
It stands and gives a fierce stare
Without any warning

You weave and cut me open
Making chronic urinary and pelvic infections
my lifetime companions

I lay my body
You party on it
My labia minora and clitoris are extinct
Tradition dictates the role of submission to me
Making me a perfect picture of misery
I say no more!
To the barbaric barga.

Waltraud Ndagijimana

Chelimo's November

Night had descended on the small mountain village, and the moon, a silver sliver, stood high in the dark sky. The village lay in darkness.

Chelimo lay on her thin mattress in the corner of the hut. It was dark inside save for a few fine streaks of moonlight that passed through the cracks in the mud walls and made weird shapes and spots on the floor. With time, the thatch of her roof had thinned and rotted in places, and long sooty strands hung precariously from the blackened beams.

A faded bed sheet and an old blanket covered Chelimo's emaciated body. She drew them up to her chin in an effort to protect herself from the chill of the night, which was slowly creeping upon her.

Chelimo was old. Tonight, in her brittle bones she felt every day of her age. Her joints ached and cracked, and she groaned as she slowly turned over to face the worn door. With a shaky hand, she pulled a frayed headscarf over her grey hair.

Another year was coming to an end. It was already November, and this year's maize harvest was safely in the granaries. The stored food had to last a whole year. The land was exhausted, the temperatures had been low, and the granaries were not as full as in past years.

Chelimo felt with certainty that the days of her life were numbered, just as the days of the year were dwindling. She lay straining her ears for any sound in the dark night outside. No drums, no songs, no whistles could be heard. She wanted to hear the songs and the drums, coming from very far away and approaching nearer and nearer, but she could not yet hear the singers or the villagers accompanying them.

Tonight was a great night for the Sabiny. For weeks, the young girls had been preparing for 'circumcision'. Chelimo knew all that it entailed. She had gone through every ritual herself as a young girl of seventeen, a very long time ago.

She remembered that she had waited with so much anticipation for her year to arrive, particularly since realising that Mongusho was looking at her with a loving eye. His family was not one to joke about. They would never accept an uncircumcised woman in their kraal. No value was attached to such a woman. She was regarded as a prostitute, and no bride price would ever be paid for her.

An uncircumcised woman would not be allowed to climb into the granary to bring out food or to milk the precious cows, nor would she even be allowed to pick up the cow dung to smear the walls and floor of her house to make it look smart. An uncircumcised woman was simply not a woman. She did not belong.

Chelimo sighed. She knew all the bad things women could do to one another and what the biting tongues could say. Oh! How clearly she remembered the incidents at the village well when she had gone there as a child with her mother! When evening drew near, all the village women would be there, talking and gossiping while they bent over the shaft to fill their clay pots and gourds.

Only Chebet stood aside. She waited for all the other women to finish filling their pots. She was never welcome to join in the other women's evening gossip. She clearly had no position in the women's hierarchy because, unlike the rest, she was not circumcised. Her arms bore no marks of honour, and she deserved no respect. She could fill her water gourd only after all the others had gone.

Some women whispered behind Chebet's back and called her a coward, while others blamed her father, a pastor, for refusing to allow her to participate in the cultural rites when she was a girl. As a result his daughter was suffering the tribe's rejection. To the Christian preachers, 'circumcision' was barbarous, the work of the devil, and had to be uprooted. They spoke out vehemently against it.

Whenever Chelimo went to the well, she knew that she was not going to be another Chebet. She would be like the other women, courageous and strong, a woman to be proud of, and Mongusho would not be afraid to ask her to be his wife and would give her parents the bride price.

Now, in the middle of the night, Chelimo remembered Mongusho. She turned on her mattress. "Mongusho, Mongusho," she murmured in her reverie. She had never forgotten him. He had been such a handsome young man, tall and strong and so fearless. Of course he changed as he grew older, but that was much later in life.

Suddenly Chelimo's ears caught the first sound of drums moving nearer to the village, and she listened to the faint songs of the girls. They were still far away. Chelimo returned to her musing, endeavouring to bring the past closer.

How she had loved it all, the excitement of the weeks preceding the great day of her 'circumcision'! All her friends had been there, a big group of young girls full of expectation and joy as they were about to go through the same ancient ritual together. They had moved as one joyful group from village to village, escorted by a large number of village children, relatives, and friends, joining in their songs and dances, so old and yet known by everybody.

They visited every relative in the surrounding villages, and in every home there was a feast, with plenty of food and drink, because the girls were expected. Weeks of joyful singing, dancing and gathering of relatives just because of the girls' coming great day!

The girls would never leave a home without receiving a gift – a she-goat, some hens, baskets of vegetables and millet, or an envelope filled with money. Their load of gifts was heavy, but the uncles and aunts wanted to show their appreciation and wish the girls well. The village children would help carry the bounty home. Of course they had an equal share in all the festivities. What a glorious season it had been!

The song Chelimo never forgot had been repeated so many times each day:

Sinay koko
Arombe, Arombe sinya yoh
Yeye, ye yeye anu wulo
Anu wulo eeh, kasenge
Amu wulo
Oh, sabasaba,
Oh sabasaba

All the relatives would come and honour the girls on their great 'circumcision' day. It was an invitation nobody would refuse.

Chelimo could still see herself in the beautiful lesu cloth that reached her knees. It was worn only by girls about to be circumcised. Her dress was held together with a belt and fastened over her breasts with a safety pin. And most important, like all the other girls, Chelimo would be blowing the whistle that hung like a necklace around her slender neck. Like all the other girls, she blew with all her might, increasing the frenzy of the dance and the din all around them. In one hand she held a flywhisk, like all the other girls, raising it high and gesticulating with authority.

Yes, there had been magic around them in those days. The spirit of the Sabiny had been felt by everybody. How long ago it now all seemed!

Chelimo was about to fall asleep, but now the songs and the beating of the drums rose in a crescendo from hill to hill as they approached. Nobody should fall asleep that night. It was another momentous night for the Sabiny. Two years the girls had waited, and, just as Chelimo had done many years ago, they had observed all the deep-rooted customs and traditions.

Chelimo smiled to herself, remembering how excited they had been on the eve of 'circumcision'. Each family prepared its own feast, and it had to be done in the very house where their daughter was born. No fancy building could be chosen. However poor the hut where she was born, it was where she would return to have her own celebration. Oh yes, Chelimo's father had prepared a lot of food and drinks. The preparations had been going on not just for a week -- the whole year had been dominated by Chelimo's coming 'circumcision' day in November.

Yes, even the eve of 'circumcision' was unforgettable. The whole village had accompanied the candidates as they went from home to home, calling people out to walk with them. Oh, all the good food they had eaten and the excited talk that had taken place, chasing away any fear of what was going to happen! Very early in the morning, the girls' faces, hands, and feet were smeared with white clay.

Everyone knew there would be no sleep that night. The songs were rising to a high pitch, and so was the dancing -- women swinging their hips, jumping and jostling, tirelessly encouraging their younger sisters to move on fearlessly.

That night Chelimo had been beautifully groomed as the whole group of girls sat together with the old and experienced women of the clan. The words spoken that night were never to be revealed to anybody else. These were sworn secrets. Nothing that was said in those dark hours had ever crossed Chelimo's lips since that time. She had never told them to anyone. Even in the hardest hours of her life she had kept them to herself, a secret bond between herself and her tribe.

Chelimo sighed as she lay on her bed. This was another 'circumcision' eve. She could clearly hear the sounds of the singing and dancing rising from the open space in the village to her house on the hill. The excitement was reaching a fever pitch. The whistles, drums, and horns grew louder. The singing and dancing, the excitement would continue the whole night, Chelimo knew. It did not matter if it kept her awake. She did not need much sleep anymore, and her mind went back once again to the night that had changed her whole life.

The old women in the tribe had never questioned the custom of cutting away women's genitals. The practice was so deeply rooted in her culture that no questions were ever asked. Hadn't her own grandmother undergone the same procedure before Grandfather had married her? He could leave her for any length of time, secure in the knowledge that she would be faithful to him. That was what mattered to him and the clan.

Had she herself feared the knife? Chelimo tried to remember. Oh, yes, when she was taken to Atar River just as dawn was about to break on her great day. That had crystallised the reality of the hour she knew was soon coming.

She had been bathed, and then her face, hands, and legs were smeared with chyme, a greenish liquid from the stomach of a freshly slaughtered sheep. This was a ceremonial blessing. It was now only a matter of moments to the great event.

Oooh kawa chemut
Oooh kawa chemut

The girls went on singing and dancing to the ancient refrain. Climbing the embankment of the Atar River, Chelimo felt fear grip her heart, but she knew she could not show any sign of alarm, not even a fluttering of her eyelids.

Chelimo sat up in her bed as she heard the old song again, just near her hut.

Oooh kawa chemut
Oooh kawa chemut

As she sang along to herself, tears rolled down her cheeks. "Too much to remember," she thought. All her hopes and the love she had longed for on that day had seemed so close to being fulfilled.

When she had left the river with the other girls, a crowd of relatives and friends had cheered them on as they met on the main village path. Above all the other sounds, dozens of shrill whistles filled the air continuously. The girls moved toward the unroofed reed enclosure. Chelimo remembered well that her legs nearly refused to

walk through the narrow entrance, but the momentum of the fearless and eager girls behind her pushed her inside.

Oooh kawa chemut
Oooh kawa chemut

Chelimo quickly glanced around the inner court. A mat was spread
out in front of each girl. She recalled how lonely she had felt at that
moment and wondered whether all her friends felt the same. She
knew she had to be brave, not to tremble, not to cry. It would not
hurt, she told herself over and over. But it seemed that her body
could not obey her reasoning, and her knees suddenly threatened to
give way.

Still, she moved on. The old women of the tribe, who had accompanied them most of the night, showed Chelimo a place on the mat.
It was covered with rustling brown banana fibres and dry grass.
"Don't be afraid," she told herself. "You are going to enter a new
world." But she could not stop shaking.

Oooh kawa chemut
Oooh kawa chemut

Slowly, Chelimo knelt down. She lay on her back and then stretched her body out on the mat. She could still make out the silvery
clouds in the sky above her.

She cast her eyes around. She saw an old woman bending over the
first girl in the line. The girl had spread her legs far apart. The circumciser clasped a glittering knife in her hand. Chelimo held her
breath, then quickly looked away and closed her eyes.

No sound had been made, no cry was heard. Chelimo opened her
eyes again, trying to hold back a tear. She realised that in a matter
of seconds the woman would be cutting the second girl. The villagers
outside the fence were just as silent as the girls inside. They all
strained to hear any cry, even a murmur, that would reveal a coward
among the girls.

Oooh kawa chemut
Oooh kawa chemut

Chelimo had not dared to look towards the first girls in the line
again, but she knew that blood was flowing freely. The girls had been
quickly covered with pieces of cloth.

As the old woman approached, Chelimo felt rising panic, but she
forced herself to keep calm and breathe slowly in and out. Suddenly,
the old woman was upon her, spreading her legs and with a swish

of the knife Chelimo's genitals were gone. A terrible pain shot through her body, stronger than anything she had felt in her life. Nothing she had heard women say could have prepared her for the consuming hurt that shook her body. Blood was pouring from the wound. The women covered her lower body with a cloth.

Terrible waves of pain shook her, and she felt was too weak to move her head. But she also felt a fierce pride envelop her. She was now a true Sabiny woman. Suddenly the ululations rose from the crowd outside signifying that the procedure was complete.

Wosho Awosho
Pango Kaywe
Wosho Awoshoi

The ancient refrain rang out through the whole village and echoed from the hills and the valleys. The crowd cheered and sang. They continued beating their drums excitedly, clapping their hands to the rhythm. Above all, there was the shrill noise of countless whistles. The sounds of 'circumcision' ceremonies in many places echoed from one hill to another, resounding, reverberating.

Relatives came dancing into the enclosure and laid gifts near their daughters. Valuable animals were given, and many baskets filled with food and fruit. Well-wishers also brought envelopes filled with money. Chelimo remembered her mother's happy face bending over her, showing the pride that swelled her heart. Oh, yes, even now, in her old age, she could still relive every minute of that day!

Wosho Awosho
Pango Kaywe
Wosho Awoshoi

The song had gone on and on. While the minutes ticked slowly away, the old women encouraged the girls to slowly stand up and move over to the seclusion hut that had been prepared for them, where they would be looked after for three days, being pampered with good food and porridge. No visitor would be allowed for those three days.

And so the first girls had slowly stood up, some bent over with pain, but even they courageously moved on towards their rough bed in the hut. Chelimo tried to rise from her mat, but she felt she had no control over her body. She lay back slowly and closed her eyes to rest. As her friends, one by one, left her behind in the enclosure, she felt helpless. She knew there was something terribly wrong with her. Pain was eating her up, searing her insides like a burning iron.

She reached out for a drink that was being passed around in a gourd. The cool water ran like a stream of life down her parched throat. She groaned and tried to sit up again, but had to lie back down.

Wosho Awosho
Pango Kaywe
Wosho Awoshoi

The dancing and singing went on relentlessly, all the village women joining in with joy and vigour. But Chelimo lay still while her friends passed by her in single file, holding their blood-stained cloths tightly around their loins.

Eventually two old women, scolding Chelimo for weakness, came to help her stand up. Chelimo desperately tried to hold the cloth around her body to cover her nakedness. She wanted to walk under her own power, but her legs gave way, and she held on to the women with the little strength that remained in her body. The women dragged her to the recovery hut.

Wosho Awosho
Pango Kaywe
Wosho Awoshoi

The other girls recovered slowly but steadily over the next few days on a special diet of well-prepared meals, roasted meat, and porridge, but Chelimo lay flat on her back for many weeks. From the day of her 'circumcision' she was never able to use her legs again.

Never did she go to the river or the well to join the other women in their evening gossip or work in the gardens together. And of course Mongusho, her love, never married her.

As she lay on her bed that night many years later, listening to yet another group of girls going for their 'circumcision', she passed her hands over her lifeless legs. She rubbed them vigorously, but she never felt even the slightest tingling.

Chelimo bent her head in a silent prayer to her Maker. Her tears flowed freely. "Oh God, please, let this not happen to any one of them! Oh God, please, let it not happen to any one of them!"

Wosho Awosho
Pango Kaywe
Wosho Awoshoi

Barbara Oketta

Pruning

And when they spoke,
It was an ORDER,
A decree
A dogma
No amount of plea would change it.
The flower had to be cut
They cut it!
Now I feel empty
Void
Nothing
The promised pride
Evades me

Cathy Anite

Crossroads

A number of hours traveling across the eastern districts of Uganda in pursuit of knowledge about the much-debated subject of female 'circumcision' takes me to Sipi Falls, in Kapchorwa. It is a beautiful area with a culturally intact community. The bold stares and glares I attract indicate that an intruder has been sighted in the area. After a few interactions, however, I realise that the people of Kapchorwa can be in fact warm-hearted and welcoming. I get myself acquainted with the folks, but I am still disturbed by the cultural beliefs and norms I have heard about. I ask myself, if the people are so gentle and loving, why the crude cultural attitude towards the female gender?

I set out to understand the Sabiny culture first, before listening to the women's voices and learning about their experiences. Claudia, of the Reproductive, Educative and Community Health (REACH) programme, was ready to support my understanding of female 'circumcision' in Kapchorwa. She explained the tradition to me and later directed me to prospective interviewees. Juliet Chemutai was one of them.

Despite the scorching afternoon sun, Juliet Chemutai stands in the compound of the small building that houses the headquarters of REACH in Kapchorwa town. She is a short, stout woman who looks around impatiently until I walk up to her and introduce myself as the interviewer. Then she beams, and we walk towards a narrow veranda where we decide to hold the interview.

Chemutai is currently part of the sensitisation group in Kapchorwa that is teaching people about the dangers of female genital mutilation. She is a thirty-two-year-old office worker, married with three children, two of them girls. The eldest is twelve years old.

As we build rapport, I ask her whether she has undergone female genital mutilation. After an uncomfortable moment of silence, she raises her head shyly and almost inaudibly answers, "No, I have not." Playing with the folds of her flowered dress, she goes on. "I am not yet cut, but I am contemplating having it done at the end of this year, in December. You know, this practice is done only during even years," she adds.

I am a little bit puzzled, so I ask her why she has chosen 2008 to be circumcised, since about twenty years have passed in which she could have been cut.

Chemutai looks at me silently. Then she asks me why she should trust me enough to talk to me about herself and her people. I reassure her by explaining my role as an interviewer and FEMRITE's good intentions. After several minutes, she tells me she is busy that day but could see me sometime later. We agree on the days to meet.

At our first meeting, Chemutai begins telling me her story, without her former reservations.

"I am going to tell you the story of my life and how sad it has made me," she begins. "As a teenager I was always under pressure to undergo 'circumcision', but I always resisted. Now I want to do it because after I got married, my in-laws, especially my mother-in-law, began insulting me and intimidating me all the time, which spoilt my mood and made me feel awful. Can you believe that I have to bear abuse and constant complaints about how useless and ill-mannered my mother is because she failed to initiate her daughter into womanhood? I cannot stand being referred to as a little girl and a disgrace to society. I am tired of the humiliation and the disrespect I get from my in-laws.

"My husband, on the other hand, is against the practice and insists that I should just turn a deaf ear and ignore his parents' insults. I am trying to persuade him to let me undergo 'circumcision' so that I can please my in-laws and be permitted to climb into the granary to get food."

"What has climbing into the granary got to do with it?" I ask, a little puzzled by the reference.

"You see, an uncircumcised woman is not supposed to go into the granary, among many other things she is not supposed to do. Can you imagine? I always have to call my neighbours' daughters who have been cut to help me get food from my own granary. It is humiliating. Sometimes I have to wait hours for them to come around, or find someone else who is circumcised to get the food from the granary for me. I am embarrassed when my mother-in-law disparages me in front of the neighbours and even my very own children.

"My father had four wives, with whom he produced ten daughters, but only three of the lot have undergone 'circumcision'. My mother also does not approve of my decision to be cut. I am aware of the post-'circumcision' complications, and my mother reminds me that it is an extremely painful experience that most of the time leads to complications during childbirth.

"I also know that I will not enjoy sex after my clitoris has been cut off, but I am willing to take my chances in exchange for dignity and respect from my in-laws. The fact that my sexual life would become a nightmare after 'circumcision' is less important than my acceptance as a full woman by my in-laws and society as a whole. My life would start a whole new chapter."

At this point Chemutai seems lost in thought, perhaps of the new life she is about to embark upon. Eventually, she continues her narrative.

"Actually, I am the second wife. My husband had another woman before me whom he left because she had been cut. He told me that he never enjoyed sex with her because it was painful for her. They would fight over sex all the time, and the woman would cry. Finally she told him to find another woman. That is the reason, I think, he does not want me to get cut -- because sex will be painful. But how can I go on being abused by my mother-in-law? She makes me feel useless.

"You know, I am so confused right now I don't know what to do. Thinking of the pain of the cutting and of the expenses I have to incur during the preparations is driving me crazy. I will have to brew a lot of beer and prepare a feast for a whole lot of people, which will definitely exhaust my financial resources. A sack of millet costs 80,000 shillings, and a sack of maize costs 50,000, and I need about four sacks. I also have to buy meat. If I finally decide to take the risk of being cut, I might be able to avoid making a big celebration and only entertain my husband's brothers and my uncles because custom obliges me to.

"My sister was circumcised at the age of fifteen. Her friends convinced her to go for 'circumcision', and she gave in owing to peer pressure. She tried to convince me too, but I refused. She started practising for the dance, and my parents prepared a party for her. When I refused to join her, she told me that I would remain a little girl, unlike herself. She would become a real woman after the ceremony. An innocent child, just a young girl, she was taken away to be cut. She suffered severe pain and fainted when she was circumcised. When she recovered, her attitude towards everyone had changed. She hated everyone and was moody all the time. After she returned home, she was never the same.

"When my sister gained enough strength to talk about her ordeal, she spoke about it with so much anger and warned me never to go for 'circumcision'. She said that when they entered the mentor's house, they were taken into a very dark room and told the Sabiny cultural secrets, which they were never to reveal to anyone. If they did, they would go mad and die. Outside the hut, meanwhile, there was dancing and drinking and unrestrained celebrating. My sister said she had no premonition about the nightmare that would change her life and haunt her forever.

"At dawn, the girls who were to be circumcised were taken to the place that had been ritually prepared. The candidates were made to lie down on their backs. Before they were cut, the circumciser warned them not to show any cowardice. If they were not brave, they would never be allowed to marry able-bodied men. When my sister's turn came, she felt the sharp blade slice through her genitals and blood come gushing out. She described the pain as so excruciating that she thought she was going to die.

"'I could not put up any fight, I could not even pretend. The pain was excruciating, unbearable. I was cut badly, and I lost a lot of blood. All the women who took part in mutilating us were half-drunk with alcohol and other drugs. They all seemed to be in a trance or lost in the world of spirits. It hurt a lot that the crowd outside danced and sang while we girls were being mutilated,' my sister told me later.

"After the operation, she said she felt helpless, abandoned in her pain and anguish when the circumciser and mentor told her to get up and walk. She was dizzy from the pain. Some herbs were crushed and the liquid from them put on her wound. Urinating became another nightmare. As the urine ran over the wound, it caused fresh pain. My sister said she tried to withhold her urine for fear of the terrible pain.

"She felt that to let your own daughter go through such suffering was nothing but evil. My sister felt unloved by her own family since they did not warn her of the outcome of the whole process. Of course she was not given any anaesthesia during the operation to reduce the pain or any antibiotics to fight infection. She believes this practice is evil and demeaning to women. She does not want any of her sisters to go through it. She would like to be the last one ever to go through what she considers such a disgusting process, and she lives only to testify against female genital cutting and fight it.

"Sometimes I sit down and think that as a woman I possess great virtues, and one of them is the ability to live life for myself and not just for the pleasure of others. Fortunately or unfortunately, my in-laws have reached the peak of their lives and soon will be gone. If I get circumcised just to please them, I will suffer the consequences alone and in vain. People should understand that traditional culture can be preserved without mutilating women's genitals. I am under so much pressure, but my feeling is that I should invest my money in a more fruitful venture than preparing for my own 'circumcision'.

"If I defy my husband's orders and go for 'circumcision', it will be the end of my marriage. If I claim to love him and enjoy having sex with him, then I should listen to him and respect his advice not to get cut, for the sake of our marriage and our children.

"If you people who come to Kapchorwa are to help us save our-selves from this savage custom, you should convince our mothers-in-law that the Creator knew what he was doing. Let them stop harassing us. The more I think of my mother-in-law's torments, the more I want to go for 'circumcision'. But the more I think about my own welfare, the more I hate the thought of being cut and want to resist it. I am at crossroads, but I think I know where the bigger force lies." As she concludes her story, her eyes dance beyond the horizon. I follow them in an attempt to detect where the bigger force lies, but the secret is hidden in her beautiful eyes.

"Today, 'circumcision' is even irrelevant," she adds thoughtfully. "There are various theories behind the history of FGC in Kapchorwa. Some say that 'circumcision' was adopted while the Sabiny were in Abyssinia and the Sudan, and the reason was that the Sabiny men wanted to reduce the sexual desire of their women while they were away on long expeditions finding pasture for their cattle. When the men returned after a couple of years or so, they sometimes found that their women had become pregnant by other men. That brought the elders to their feet, and they finally convened a meeting and came up with the scheme of lowering the sexual desire of their women. They tricked the women into believing that the practice was meant to initiate girls into womanhood. Today our husbands are here with us most of the time, and there is no way we are going to have children fathered by other men.

"Another theory goes that since the Sabiny were originally pastoralists, they had numerous ways of treating their animals. If an animal fell sick, they would cut part of the neck and bleed it, and it would get well without other treatment. So the men thought that if they cut and bled a certain body part of their women, it would boost their immunity to illness. This started the elders thinking about which part of the body to cut. The ear and neck were too visible. So they decided that the labia and clitoris were better options because they were in a 'secret location,' and it would be difficult to notice whether or not they were cut. This theory too is irrelevant since hospitals and clinics are now available to help all of us.

"Still another theory is that the Sabiny forefathers ordered 'circumcision' of women because they wanted to get rid of the offensive smells that women's genitals emitted. Living as they did in semi-arid areas, where there was always a water shortage and none could be spared for washing, cutting off the genitals was intended to substitute for hygiene. Of course, this idea no longer applies either because Kapchorwa is blessed with water."

As Juliet alludes to the abundance of water, I look across the green field toward the roaring Sipi Falls and agree. Kapchorwa is well endowed. It is unbelievable that the same beautiful Kapchorwa throws women into a quagmire, entrapping them in endless pain and joyless existence. Here tradition is placed above the individual, the family above the woman.

Another angle is more interesting. For many women in other cultures, 'circumcision' is seen as the mechanism that liberates the female body from its masculine properties and is thus seen as a source of empowerment and strength. But must the price of empowerment be robbery in broad daylight?

Margaret Ntakalimaze

Her Last Word

The long-awaited time of the year
For becoming a woman has come
Whispered Musuya to Masawe
They are on standby
Waiting for the drums and songs to start
Then it's heard at a distance
The girls shiver and their hearts rage
Holding their hands tightly
They pray to God for courage
Unlike the Sabiny women
They are afraid
Afraid of the unknown
Yet
Becoming a woman indeed they must.
Yonder there is the river.
A place of miracles
They join other girls all decorated with
white-and-brown dotted lines
Covering their faces and stomachs
Their heads are shaven in a style
Only for the women-to-be
Braving the chilly dawn
Eee ... ho ho!
They are singing and dancing to the tunes of
the drums
Aloft a woman tightly holds a metallic blade
It's glistering in the air
Her stomach moves in and out as she dances
She stamps her feet vigorously on the ground
Her eyes spitting fire
She is in a different world
Perhaps talking to her ancestors
Seeking guidance and blessings
Then she halts

Calling them one by one – she starts her job
The metallic blade like a tongue licks human flesh
Becoming a woman indeed they must
Musuya, Musuya, it is your turn, Masawe whispers
Be courageous my dear
Remember our beloved men are waiting for us
Soon we shall be in their arms
And that is what we long for
So be it.
Don't disappoint them
Becoming a woman indeed we must
Holding the metallic blade tightly
The woman looks at Musuya with a frozen face
She quickly fastens her hands on her womanhood
The sharpened blade tearing her apart
Merciless!
Blood gushes out
Her eyes are wild with fear
Masawe pats her shoulder
We are now women among the Sabiny
A tribe with a difference …
Stop the nonsense
It's Musuya's turn to speak
Don't you feel the pain?
Is that the difference?
Why should any woman do this?
Has it made you a woman?
What makes you woman has been chopped off?
That part that makes us… us… women
No, no, stop it!
She pants as she slides to the ground
And breathes her last.

Betty Kituyi

My Mbasuben

With my writer friends I am enjoying the pleasant ambience of the green Kapchorwa hills from the backyard of Marsha Hotel. It is hard to believe that we are finally here. Our journey, which began simply in a *matatu* that had just been relieved of its load of Irish potatoes and chickens at Nakawa Taxi Park in Kampala, finally brought us to this place with its breath-taking beauty.

The hotel sits atop a hill and gives you the feeling that you are eating at the table of a mountain. From where we are seated, we can stretch our necks and look down upon the vehicles snaking along a narrow road, several hundred metres below, that divides a fertile valley. Small yellow wildflowers, typical of Mount Elgon's fertility, add to the magnificent diversity of the place. The people of Kapchorwa greet us with warm but inquiring smiles. They can tell we are strangers, and they quickly ask where we are from and why we are here. Otherwise, they seem at peace with themselves in their serene environment.

In the dying glow of the sun and the growing shadows of the cold evening, we wonder whether the happiness of the Kapchorwa people stems from their generous natural environment, or from their secrets, like those told to the 'circumcision' candidates on the night before they are cut. The fresh, clean air of this place is not a force for cultural understanding but produces a shivering question: why would a people living in such a sanctified climate indulge in the harmful ancient practice of female genital mutilation (FGM), which maims their womenfolk.

Kapchorwa is one of the districts in Uganda where the Sabiny live and practice FGM. They have also settled in other districts nearby, around Mount Elgon, maintaining the tradition wherever they live. My colleagues and I have come to talk to some Sabiny women who are willing to volunteer information about their experiences with FGM.

Nothing had prepared me for the energy, enthusiasm, and fire displayed by the young woman I interviewed. She was a proud 'circumcision' candidate for the upcoming December 2008 season. Our meeting took place in the compound of the REACH programme's office in Kapchorwa town, where we sat, with the mountain birds twittering in the background.

Brenda Cherop is a beautiful young woman with light, flawless, apple-smooth skin. Her eyes have a rare brown tint and glimmer with joy. The sparkle in them is that of a woman who has not felt a lot of pain in her life. She smiles easily. I am immediately enchanted by her natural beauty. She says she wants to be cut because, in addition to relieving the pressure from her mother-in-law, she wants to have a *mbasuben*.

"When you are circumcised in a group, you get one strong friend known as *mbasuben*," she says. Her father has got a *mbasuben*, the boy candidate who stood before him in the 'circumcision' line, which was arranged according to the candidates' fathers' ages.

"When he invites him for a visit to our home, my father slaughters a sheep for a feast as a sign of respect. When his *mbasuben's* children are 'circumcision' candidates and come singing, dancing, chest to knee, and swishing an ox-tail fly whisk in the air, my father ensures that they relax in a chair while he showers them with gifts. Sometimes he gives them goats, sometimes a cow or a bull," Brenda says. "Unfortunately for my father, he has not had any of his own children circumcised so far, since I am his first-born child, and therefore his *mbasuben* has never repaid in kind what my father has given him."

Brenda feels guilty about the fact that she and her siblings have not given their father the opportunity to win his mbasuben's respect. She is obsessed with getting herself a *mbasuben* of her own. The interviews that I had held earlier, with other women, had not indicated that a woman was willing to sacrifice her womanhood in order to form a strong friendship with another woman. Listening to Brenda, it is clear that a *mbasuben* is an important and enduring non-kin friendship and a source of support that is greatly treasured by the Sabiny. Brenda's desire to be accepted and recognised as a fully committed adult member of her community is quite evident in her talk. But after hours of hearing her words, resonant with passion for 'circumcision', one gets the feeling that she is a victim of another cultural attitude and is not aware of the danger 'circumcision' presents to her and other women in her society. Brenda Cherop's thirst for the knife generally represents the views of other young women concerning the FGM practice in Kapchorwa.

"If you belonged to the circles of my mother and my grandmothers, who have all been cut, you would understand the urge deeply embedded in me, to do it just as they did. In the eyes of the Sabiny, I am a girl and not a woman, even though I am married and the mother of two children. When my neighbour comes to my home to borrow an axe to split her firewood and I am somewhere in the house where she cannot see me, she calls, 'Have you seen the girl?' I find that so insulting. For how long will I be called chepta kai (the girl of this home)? Between my five-year-old daughter and me, there is no cultural difference. Eyes follow me whenever I go to the shops to buy salt, matches, or tea leaves. Often I catch people laughing at me and speaking in whispers when they see me, as if they are saying, 'That's Martin's wife, she is a chepta kai.' They would sooner give respect to a fly falling in the visiting mbasuben's chicken soup than to me.

"The secrets of the 'circumcision' night are a mystery to everyone who has not undergone 'circumcision'. The candidates go to the river escorted by women who have already been circumcised. The girls strip naked to bathe in the cold, biting waters in the grey morning, to gain strength and to numb the pain when the time comes for the cutting. There are things the mentors tell them. We are told an animal comes by and makes four marks on their right arms. No one is supposed to tell the secrets to anyone who is not circumcised. It is believed that if she dares, the 'circumcision' spirits will hound her forever. I do not want to be excluded from my tribe's secrets, since I am a Sabiny. Sometimes people say, 'What if there are no secrets and those elders just lie to lure you to do it?' But you see, I want to find out for myself.

"I am aware that these are changing times and that this is an old custom. Some people are denouncing it, but they are looking at it from outside the community. How are we supposed to deal with the crushing views of those in the family, the immediate people we live with? My mother-in-law will use any small excuse to remind me that I am a senseless girl. When my two young children play with her banana leaves and spoil them, her banana plantation being near our house, she says they have no sense because their mother is not circumcised. She introduces my daughter to her friends as 'the daughter of the uncircumcised girl,' and then my daughter asks me tearfully, 'Mummy, what is wrong with Kukhu (Grandmother)? Why does she call you chepta kai?' What am I supposed to tell my daughter when my mother-in-law jeers at me for cowardice?

"My husband, Martin, also wants me to be cut. He is circumcised and I am not. According to the tribe, I should be taboo to him. I have been married to him for five years now. I was a 'circumcision' candidate the year that I discovered that I was pregnant with his child. We girls had been dancing for two weeks when I began vomiting every time we sang erotic songs. We went to bathe together in the river at cockcrow, but when I poured water from a calabash over my body, a sour-milk taste would rise in my mouth and I would start shivering violently as if possessed by some spirits. Rumours spread in my circle of aunties that I showed the signs of becoming a circumciser in the future. They began treating me with respect, and it was decided that I would be the first in the line we would form in my father's courtyard, which also coincided with my father's being the eldest among the candidates' fathers.

"As 'circumcision' day drew closer and we continued dancing, from Kaserem to Sipi, Nyenge, Kaptwanya, Tegeres and other villages, I became dizzier with each dance step. We had to rehearse many times to perfect the dance. Sometimes I fainted. Still, they believed that I had the special powers of the 'circumcision' spirits. I was confused and scared about what was happening to me.

"One night when we were dancing outside the home of one of the girls, I noticed the new moon, looking very delicate, as if it were about to roll off the clouds. Just then, one of the mentors sang and urged all the girls to look up and enter the moon and be cleansed in its clear waters before the 'circumcision' weekend. Normally, my monthly period coincided with the appearance of the new moon. My heart missed a beat when I remembered that exactly one month earlier, Martin and I had been intimate.

"During the next moments, instead of feeling the warmth that flows down my back just before my menstrual period begins, I felt betrayed by the moon and felt the chill of the cold evening for the first time. I was pregnant! I could not imagine facing the scrutiny of the mentors and circumcisers. I could not go through the ceremony when I was in this condition. It was a taboo. Besides, it could also be dangerous to me and my baby. I kept this knowledge to myself through the night.

"The following day, I looked for Martin at his shop and found him weighing maize flour for a customer. He was surprised to see me because he knew I was supposed to be dancing with the other village girls. After his customer had gone, I sat down on the wooden bench where his customers sit to drink soda. When he asked how I was, I told him that I was pregnant. He rolled his tongue over his teeth, ran to me, lifted my face in his hands, and kissed me.

"'That is very good news!' he shouted.

"His kiss did not erase the realisation that my life had taken a new turn. I had got off the narrow path of my education onto a wider road of marriage and children. I was nineteen years old and would have been a Senior Four candidate at Kapchorwa Senior Secondary School the following year. I loved to study, and my intention had been to become one of the few female doctors in our district. I was very good at sciences. Besides, I felt too young to be a mother.

"'What will happen to my education?' I asked him."

"'Don't worry, my sweetheart, education is good but having a child is better,' he answered.

"I told him that I wanted to abort the child so that I could continue with my education since the school would not let me study if I was pregnant.

"'If that is what you want, then my auntie, who is a midwife in Kenya, will help you to terminate the pregnancy,' he said. That comforted me for a while. I thought it would be very easy to end the pregnancy.

"Because I feared to be confronted by my family and the law and the danger the circumciser's knife would put me through, he convinced me to elope with him to Kenya that night. I did not have time to go home. The moon hid behind the clouds that night, and we fled as the enchanting girls' voices were being swallowed up by the roaring Sipi Falls behind us.

"My aroused 'circumcision' spirit was quickly hushed by the silence of the sleeping hills as we walked out of Kapchorwa. I wished that the Sipi Falls could sweep us downstream smoothly and quickly to our destination, but instead we had to endure hours of nose-wrinkling stench from chicken droppings as we crouched between bunches of bananas and other produce on a lorry headed for the border town of Malaba.

"In Malaba, we stayed in a place called Kongoni, where Martin's auntie lived. Five days later, Martin had changed his mind about my having an abortion. He spoke like one of those old men in our village back home when he said, 'I cannot use my money to kill my own seed.' Then I realised that he had tricked me. I felt betrayed at first, but when I saw how supportive and loving he was, I decided to bring forth our child.

"I delivered a healthy, beautiful baby girl with round cheeks. We stayed in Kenya for two years, and we were happy. Martin was able to open another small grocery shop where we were living. No one cared whether I was circumcised or not. We were mixed in with people from Bantu tribes, who do not circumcise, although some of our neighbours were from sister tribes like the Kalenjin, the Nandi, and Pokot, who shared our ancestry.

"When we came back to Kapchorwa after two years, the bubble surrounding my world burst, and I was rudely reminded of my cultural obligations. People called me a disgraceful, cowardly girl who had fled the knife. I was hit with the Sabiny reality that the pain I bit between my teeth during the birth of my children did not qualify as a rite of passage to becoming a full woman in my tribe. It became clear that I would not be beautiful to my husband until the hidden parts of my girlhood were seized and cut away by the sharp knife, under public scrutiny in the name of courage. Even if he doesn't say so, sometimes I wonder whether Martin finds me unclean. Shall we reach another level of sexual satisfaction after I get cut? I also know that my getting cut will win him the respect of his friends and clansmen."

What Brenda doesn't know is that her sexual and reproductive life will never be the same after she is circumcised. Only a few circumcised women can lead a relatively normal sexual life and reach orgasm. Most women who have been cut experience difficulty in having sex, especially as they get older, and that puts a lot of strain on their marriages. Owing to sexual frustration, their husbands often acquire a younger wife. Only a handful of men in Kapchorwa have only one wife. The rest just keep marrying and marrying.

Brenda reveals that she enjoys having sex with her husband and they have a healthy, fulfilling sex life. She agrees that the parts she is willing to sacrifice in the upcoming December 'circumcision' are essential for sexual pleasure. I tell her what a district official told me while in the matatu from Kampala bound for this hilly spot: 'The men say amongst themselves that they find uncut girls too passionate, demanding a lot of time and energy, engaging them the whole night. They prefer brief but enchanting sexual episodes with the pain-stricken circumcised women.' Brenda and I agree that female 'circumcision' is the social regulation of sexual desire among women.

Admiring Brenda's beauty, I cannot help thinking that her husband might be feeling insecure and therefore worried that she might attract other men and cheat on him whenever he is away on business. To control her, he may want her to be circumcised so that he can be the only one to have her. When I tell her this, she is surprised and seems confused.

She has heard that circumcised women have difficulty during childbirth, but a mentor challenged that idea and told Brenda that Caesareans were most frequent among uncircumcised women. According to the mentor, the false allegations that 'circumcision' causes problems in delivery are just spread by people who hate Sabiny culture. She told Brenda that the reason Caesarean deliveries never occurred in the past among Sabiny women was because every girl was circumcised then. It occurs to me that the mentors and circumcisers are past masters at indoctrination. Unfortunately, Brenda seems to trust most the authority and opinions of the cultural leaders.

Brenda has had very little exposure to the community outside her home. She spends most of her time caring for her two children. She does not meet other women to talk about issues that affect them.

Brenda's mbasuben-obsessed mind does contain the question of why her mother-in-law does not live with her father-in-law. Brenda only knows that the woman has been separated from the father of her children for many years now. Brenda's intoxication with the idea of 'circumcision' seems to blind her to the fact that women of her mother-in-law's age group (fifty and above) do not want to have sex with their husbands. At that age, they experience serious pain with sex, and most of them opt out of their marriages altogether.

Brenda's obsession with belonging to the group and being recognised as a gendered and participating member of her society outweighs acknowledgment of the pain, and the health and psychological implications of 'circumcision'. Brenda and the other young women of Kapchorwa need to think past the issue of belonging.

At twenty-four years of age, Brenda has her whole life ahead of her. She realises that the Sabiny are no longer pastoralists but are now farmers. Still, her obsession with culture seems to defeat her rationality. She is determined to be a 'circumcision' candidate come December. The mentors have been thorough. I feel she has been brainwashed, and it seems to be my duty to do something to help her regain her senses. But what can I do? She now tells me more about preparations for her initiation ceremony.

"Five years ago, I joined the 'circumcision' group out of sheer excitement and love of dancing, enticed by the erotic songs sung by my age-sets (punda or dwowo) such as Fungua siliwale fungua haa (Open your knickers, open knickers). 'Circumcision' time is the only time young people get away with speaking obscenities. In a crowd, one can say anything. But because of my escapades with Martin, I did not go forward with the cutting then.

"This time around, my motivation to do it is different. They have abused me to the point where I am now strong. When you have gained courage like I have now, your energy flows into preparing other things that accompany the ceremony. It is a simple ceremony. Two months away from the event, I am preparing the millet and maize to make beer (komeka teshonik). My people will drink that. They drink to forget the pain of their daughters when the shadows grow long on the 'circumcision' day.

"The elders sit on small wooden chairs around a pot and suck up the brew through special long straws. We shall make tea for the teetotallers. I may have the 'circumcision' in my home and not at my father's. I am allowed that choice. My home is very near my father's home, so it really doesn't matter much. Besides, this is the first time so many people will be invited to my home. It is such an honour. My sister is preparing to be circumcised with me. Other candidates can join us if they wish.

"I am still waiting for school to close after the students have finished their examinations so that together we can start rehearsing the songs. It is going to be a joyous occasion accompanied by chants, ululations, and the vulgar 'circumcision' songs. We shall sing through the night, going from one relative's home to another. I will tie a lesu cloth around my neck and let it fly as I dance. The lesu covers the ordinary clothes beneath it and signifies a woman of valour. I will fasten a belt around my stomach for strength. I will also hold a cow's-tail whisk and swing it as part of the dignifying regalia accompanying my dance steps.

"Very early on the morning of 'circumcision', we shall bathe in the cold water to numb our bodies to the anticipated pain. Holding the whisk firmly in my hands and raising it above my abdomen, at the same time lying flat on a sand-sprinkled sisal sack, I will open my eyes wide and never blink as the circumciser bends to cut me. I will display my courage to the many witnesses and show that I do not fear the knife. I know that it is going to be painful since it is done without any anaesthetic, but that will be viewed as a test of my courage. Bravery and self-control during the operation are integral parts of Sabiny personhood, and I am ready to show that I possess them.

"I am looking forward to seeing the smiles on my grandmother's face, exposing the gaps in her lower teeth. Women of her generation had their lower teeth drilled out. My grandmother has been gently encouraging me to go for 'circumcision' all along. Knowing that the custom of her mother and grandmother before her has been passed on to my generation and that of my daughter, she can die peacefully.

"I think that on that day, my mother-in-law will finally be satisfied. I imagine her dancing with a kiset (oval traditional basket) full of presents -- a bottle of honey, ghee, a lesu, and other things -- while leading the people marching in a line to offer gifts to celebrate and congratulate me on my courage and welcome me into the tribe's much-cherished womanhood. I think my mother-in-law will become my best friend, because my not being circumcised so far has been the only thing standing between us.

"My husband is likely to keep quiet and be contented, now that everything is in place. My father too will feel proud and will regain status in the community. Most important, he will get gifts from his mbasuben."

Whatever the outcome, Brenda is determined to brave the knife. I share a few stories I have gathered from my other interviews. I tell her of the laments of Milcah, the thirty-eight-year-old mother of four from Bukwo, who exclaims, "Those people cut my body for nothing! If I had known the truth I would not have undergone it. These four tribal 'circumcision' marks on my skin mark me out as less human, less of a woman! It is a humiliation, a betrayal." Milcah told me that she had experienced a lot of pain giving birth. Her 'circumcision' wound had healed improperly, stretching the skin on her inner thigh, which tore when she was pushing in delivering her baby. The pain she felt was more than labour pains. Brenda does not seem to hear me. The mentors have done their job. Her courage becomes my pain.

After several meetings, Brenda agreed to visit REACH and talk to the women and men in those offices. REACH started in 1996 in Kapchorwa town, to promote the rights of every woman, man, girl and boy, and enable them to enjoy lives of good health and equal opportunities, using a culturally sensitive approach. I convinced Brenda to go to REACH because I believed that she would be told more truthful stories, some of which might dissuade her from going for 'circumcision'. She will find out more facts about the effects of FGM and how it is likely to change her life completely afterwards.

Brenda promises me that she will surely weigh all sides of the situation. She shakes my hand and turns to leave. I am not quite sure, but I think there is a new twist in her voice. I hang on to this hope, that she will evaluate the consequences of FGM for her psychological, social, spiritual and physical wellbeing. I hope that she can find a strong mbasuben in other activities that weave women's experiences together, such as childbirth, parenting, singing, or joining the visiting circles that thrive in her community.

It then occurs to me that an alternative rite of passage by the Sabiny community could be sought. I quickly call Brenda back and tell her so. I remember that in one of the tribes in Kenya, they have resorted to circumcising their girls through words instead of the knife. They have maintained the week of seclusion that used to follow 'circumcision', and they use it to give lessons on adult life. This is a joint effort by rural families and the Kenyan national women's group, Maendeleo ya Wanawake Organisation. This might be emulated by the Sabiny.

Epilogue

A month after I interviewed Brenda, I talked to a REACH official and inquired about Brenda and whether she was still determined to be cut. The news that Claudia gave me brought tears of joy to my eyes. Brenda had made the right decision. December had come and gone, leaving her uncircumcised, a complete woman. Her desire now was to go back to school and complete her education if she could raise the school fees.

Maryam Sheikh Abdi

The Cut

I was only six years old
when they led me to the bush, to my slaughterhouse.
Too young to know what it all entailed,
I walked lazily towards the waiting women.

Deep within me was the desire to be cut,
as pain was my destiny:
it is the burden of femininity,
so I was told.
Still, I was scared to death . . .
but I was not to raise the alarm.

The women talked in low tones,
each trying to do her tasks the best.
There was the torso-holder,
she had to be strong to hold you down.
Legs and hands each had their own woman,
who needed to know her task
lest you free yourself and flee for life.

The cutting began with the eldest girl
and on went the list.
Known to be timid, I was the last among the six.
I shivered and shook all over;
butterflies beat madly in my stomach.
I wanted to vomit, the waiting was long,
the expectation of pain too sharp,
but I had to wait my turn.
My heart pounded, my ears blocked;
the only sound I understood
was the wails from the girls,
for that was my destiny as well.
Finally it was my turn, and one of the women
winked at me:

Come here, girl, she said, smiling unkindly.
You won't be the first nor the last,
but you have only this once to prove you are brave!
She stripped me naked. I got goose pimples.
A cold wind blew, and it sent warning signs
all over me. I choked, and my head
went round in circles as I was led.

Obediently, I sat between the legs of the woman
who would hold my upper abdomen,
and each of the other four women grasped my legs and hands.
I was stretched apart and each limb firmly held.
And under the shade of a tree . . .
The cutter begun her work . . .
the pain . . . is so vivid to this day,
decades after it was done.
God, it was awful!

I cried and wailed until I could cry no more.
My voice grew hoarse, and the cries could not come out,
I wriggled as the excruciating pain ate into my tender flesh.
Hold her down! cried the cursed cutter,
and the biggest female jumbo sat on my chest.
I could not breathe, but there was nobody
to listen to me.
Then my cries died down, and everything was dark.
As I drifted, I could hear the women laughing,
joking at my cowardice.

It must have been hours later when I woke up
to the most horrendous reality.
The agonizing pain was unbearable!
It was eating into me, every inch of my girlish body was aching.
The women kept exchanging glances
and talked loudly of how I would go down in history,
as such a coward, until I fainted in the process.
Allahu Akbar! they exclaimed as they criticised me.
I looked down at myself and got a slap across my face.
Don't look, you coward, came the cutter's words;

then she ordered the women to pour hot sand on my cut genitals.
My precious blood gushed out and foamed.
Open up, snarled the jumbo woman, as she poured the sand on
me.
Nothing they did eased the pain.

Ha! How will you give birth? taunted the one with the smile.
I was shaking and biting my lower lip.
I kept moving front, back, and sideways as I writhed in pain.
This one will just shame me! cried the cutter.
Look how far she has moved, how will she heal?
My sister was embarrassed, but I could see pain in her eyes . . .
maybe she was recalling her own ordeal.
She pulled me back quickly to the shed.

The blood oozed and flowed.
Scavenger birds were moving in circles
and perching on nearby trees.
Ish! Ish!, the women shooed the birds.
All this time the pain kept coming in waves,
each wave more pronounced than the one before it.

The women stood us up but warned us not to move our legs apart.
They scrubbed the bloody sand off our thighs and small buttocks,
then sat us back down.
A hole was dug,
malmal, the stick herb, was pounded;
the ropes for tying our legs were ready.
Charcoal was brought and put in the hole,
where there was dried donkey waste and many herbs;
¬these were the cutter's paraphernalia.

The herbs were placed on the charcoal,
and we were ordered to sit over the hole.
As I sat with smoke rising around me,
I could hear the blood dropping on the charcoal,
and more smoke rose.
The pain was somehow dwindling but I felt weak
and nauseated.

Maybe she is losing blood? My sister asked worriedly.
No, no. It will stop once I place the herbs, cried the cutter impatiently.
The malmal was pasted where my severed vaginal lips had been,
and then I was tied from my thighs to my toes
with very strong ropes from camel hide.
A long stick was brought and the women took turns
showing us how to walk, sit, and stand.
They told us not to bend or move apart our legs¬
This will make you heal faster, they said,
but it was meant to seal up that place.

The drop of the first urine,
more burning than the aftermath of the razor,
passed slowly, bit by bit,
one drop after another,
while I lay on my side.
There was no washing, no drying,
and the burning kept on for hours later.
But there was no stool . . .
at least, I don't remember.

For the next month this was my routine.
There was no feeding on anything with oil,
or anything with vegetables or meat.
Only milk and ugali formed my daily ration.
I was given only sips of water:
This avoids "wetting" the wound and delaying healing, they said.

We would stay in the bush the whole day.
The journey from the bush back home began around four
and ended sometimes at seven.
All this time we had to face the heat
and bare-footedly slide towards home . . .
with no water, of course.
We were not to bend if a thorn struck us,
never to call for help loudly
as this would "open" us up and the cutter
would be called again.

Everything was about scary dos and don'ts.

I stayed on with the other five
for the next four weeks. None of us bathed;
lice developed between the ropes and our skin,
biting and itching the whole day and night.
There was no way to remove them,
at least not until we healed.

The river was only a kilometre away.
Every morning the breeze carried
the sweet scent of its waters to us,
making our thirst more real.

The day the cutter was called back
each of us shivered and prayed silently,
each hoping we had healed
and there would be no cutting again.
Thank God we were all done
except one unlucky girl
who had to undergo it all again,
and took months to heal.

Our heads were shaved clean.
The ropes untied, lice dropped at last.
We were showered and oiled,
but most important was the drinking of water.
I drank until my stomach was full,
but the mouth and throat yearned for more.

It was over.
All over my thighs were marks from the ropes,
dotted with patches from the lice wounds.
Now I was to look after myself,
to ensure that everything remained intact
until the day I married.

"The Cut" © 2006 Maryam Sheikh Abdi

Sophie Bamwoyeraki

Vultures of Culture

Spare feelings for the infant girl,
pinned down like a goat for slaughter
as the vultures of culture take their posture,
to define her as a member, they dismember her,
to give her identity in their society they obliterate her self-identity,
to brand her as one of their own, underhand teaching is sown.

Feel sympathy for this infant girl
whose outlook has been brainwashed
and falsehood etched on her mind.
Facts have been shrouded by deceit.
Treachery and Betrayal are her constant playmates.
She's now convinced that this operation:
will prevent her from being the scorner of family honour,
will enhance her femininity and fertility,
will expel body odour and embody a purity decoder,
will check averted behaviour and be her saviour from shame,
will cleanse her and render her acceptable.
And that this operation is urgent,
because it is her only bridge to womanhood.

Grieve for this infant girl,
As the vultures of culture
Descend upon her, their talons armed with:
Broken glass, tin lids, thorns, razor blades,
scissors, sharpened sticks and knives.
Poking, pricking, piercing, incising,
stretching, cutting and stitching.
She has cold water for anaesthesia.
Shock awaits her if she won't bear the acute pain.

Empathise with this infant girl,
For she may experience haemorrhage after the operation,
Scars and damage to the urethra.
The future may await her with poor retention of urine,
urinary tract infections and gloom at child birth.

Feel sorry for this infant girl.
Feel sorry for this infant girl,
because she stands to blame
for any permanent damage she sustains
since she kicked her leg
and distracted the hands
of the vultures of culture during the operation.
Spare feelings for the infant girl.

Hilda Twongyeirwe Rutagonya

The Intrigue

"Most husbands sodomise their circumcised wives because the wives cannot handle vaginal sexual intercourse. That has become the norm for most circumcised women. But no one talks about it. Each wife is silent. Silent so as not to shame her husband, silent so as not to shame her society, silent so as not to shame herself. It is heart-breaking. Every married woman knows that bedroom matters are very personal and very private. As I talk to you now, I feel as if I am making a confession in front of a Catholic priest. I feel as if I am undressing right in front of you. But it is okay. I want to tell you my story."

I encourage Yemo to speak. I tell her that together we have to break the silence. I tell her that it is not right that social norms continue to silence women in matters that affect them so seriously.

"I agree with you," she responds. "But these are things I have never discussed with anyone before, not even with other circumcised women. We are all silent. When I tried to talk to my mother, she just told me to be patient, she did not give me her ear. I had hoped that maybe she would share with me her own experiences. But she did not. She did not treat my question as a matter of any importance.

"'Just be patient,' she said to me, and changed the subject. She sounded as if we were not supposed to talk about it. I pressed on, but she just would not talk.

"After that attempt, I decided I would live with it silently, and that is what I have done for the ten years of my marriage. Silence. I have kept quiet and pretended that all was well. Tell me, what else could I do?"

I do not respond to Yemo because I am not sure what more she could have done. It is difficult to respond to issues about which one does not have first-hand experience. Sometimes we hurt people when we offer advice about something they know better. So I keep quiet and just listen.

Yemo and I are seated in her hotel room in Cape Town, where we have met while each of us is here on a different mission. She came on a social scientist's trip, and I am on a publisher's trip. Her friend from Ethiopia, whom I had met before, had introduced Yemo to me. As we chatted, I told Yemo of our project, recording voices of women speaking about female genital mutilation.

"'I could add my voice,' she had said matter-of-factly.

"Sure," I had responded, but I was not sure because our project was coming to an end. Indeed, Yemo's story turned out to be full-term and needed to be born.

Yemo began. "I have three young sisters. I am the first-born in our family. Fortunately, none of them is circumcised. As I looked at them growing up, I was very inquisitive, especially when we would be in the bathroom or in our bedroom getting dressed. That is when I realised that they were not like me. Sometimes my mother would ask me to help bathe them, and I would jump at the opportunity to discover them in order to discover myself. But when I discovered what I discovered, I fell silent. I did not ask anyone to explain, though I felt a strong desire to know. Later I heard about 'circumcision', and I came to know that I was circumcised. Slowly I became a very withdrawn child.

"My early childhood was not exciting at all. As we were growing up, there was a very distinct difference between my sisters and me. While I was very reserved, they were very free-spirited. Over time, my mother began referring to my 'circumcision' as if to confirm what I already knew. She would shout at my sisters and tell them that they were stubborn and badly behaved because they had not been circumcised. On the other hand, she always commended me for my calm behaviour.

"According to my mother, and maybe according to custom, I was sensible and well behaved because I was circumcised. Of course she is right. For the most part, my lack of spirit, my quietness resulted from my recognition that I was different, the knowledge that something was wrong with my womanhood. I don't hate my mother, and I know that I am my mother's favourite daughter, but I feel sad that she looked on as a knife changed my life. I fail to understand how a mother gives birth to a normal child and then offers up the child to be disabled. To tell you the truth, a great sadness sits deep in my heart. I have an anger that makes me calmer than my sisters. An anger that makes me resigned. An anger that what I should have been was taken away."

I tell Yemo that she need not be resigned, that life is about fighting to the end. I want to get up and hug her and reassure her, but I can feel the wall that she has built around herself and I respect the distance between us. Instead, I hold my hands tightly together to support my drooping chin as I listen to her small but strong voice. The wine-coloured blouse that she wears hugs her waist tightly, exposing her fine figure. She is a very beautiful woman.

"What reason do I have not to be resigned?"

Yemo almost raises her voice. She stands up, walks to the electric kettle and fixes me a cup of Five Roses tea. She serves me some tasty biscuits from a little tin sitting on her table.

"I have every reason to be resigned. I will tell you that since I got married ten years ago, I have never enjoyed sex. I still bleed every time my husband and I meet. No matter how many times we have had sex, no matter what we do, it never ceases to hurt. Tell me the truth, my sister, what brings a husband and wife together? You and I know that all other reasons that we always give are apologies for the real reason. So, tell me, why shouldn't I be resigned?

"I was circumcised when I was six months old. And my mother tells me that I was a baby of slight build.

"My great-grandfather was a medicine man. He was very influential and was believed to be very knowledgeable about almost every cultural and medical issue. That is what I was told about him. Thank God that I never met him in my adult life, but by the time I grew up, he was long dead.

"I was his first great-granddaughter and came among several great-grandsons. When I was born, the family celebrated my arrival. My great-grandfather was especially happy. As a special child, therefore, I got special and preferential treatment. I was the lucky child, and so I was to be circumcised by the renowned, knowledgeable medicine man. I was cut by my great-grandfather.

"I have always asked myself how he found and cut the tiny parts. I look at my little daughter today, and the genital parts are so small and smooth. How that man gripped and cut me when I was six months old is not comprehensible.

"My only joy comes from the fact that FGM is now a crime in Ethiopia. But of course it is still going on behind curtains. The targets are small girls and babies, who, they know, will not talk or report. At least criminalising 'circumcision' makes it easier for those who are fighting it. But there is a need to sensitise women so that they can fight for their daughters without waiting for things to go wrong, as they did for my mother and me.

"After my great-grandfather cut me, he went back to his home. He was from my mother's lineage. My father, I understand, was not aware of my 'circumcision'. My mother had hoped that she could nurse me quietly and I would be healed without my father being involved. Unfortunately for me and my mother, my wound festered. My mother gave me antibiotics, and the great medicine man also sent the best of his collection, but the infection dug deeper and wider. My mother has told me several times how she almost lost me to the infection: a tiny baby with massive, massive wounds. How, for uncounted hours, she sat and held me in her hands and cried over my tiny, formless body. How she worried I would slip through her fingers and regretted the act of 'circumcision'. Am I supposed to sympathise with her?

"After several weeks of trauma, she took me to hospital, where we spent several more weeks. The most incredible thing is that my mother's relatives said that I got the infection because I was visited by an evil spirit. The baby was blamed. They said that I had a bad omen that attracted the evil spirit. I was disgusted as I listened to my mother explaining to me about the evil spirit. She too believed it. She still believes it. As if my pain was not enough, my father also rejected me. He said that I was not his daughter since my mother and her people were doing whatever they wanted without his involvement. My mother suffered so much with me. When I finally recovered, she swore that if she had more daughters, she would never have any of them circumcised. Interestingly, my father has still not accepted me.

"'You were the sacrificial lamb,' my mother always tells me.

"When I got married, at the age of 21, I did not have the slightest idea of what lay ahead for me on my bridal bed. I had kept myself pure and had never had any sexual encounters. When my boyfriend proposed to me, I was very excited. I wanted to be his wife because I liked him a lot and we had been friends for some time. Shortly after that, he suggested that we inform our parents and seek their blessings so that they could help us to organise our wedding. We, especially he, did not want to have sexual intercourse before we were actually married, officially husband and wife. And so by the time we were wed, we wanted each other very much. I looked forward to our wedding night. I had waited for him just as he had waited for me.

"It was funny when on our wedding night we remembered that we were not supposed to share a bed. So we slept in different rooms. Our religion prohibits sex after a wedding for at least seventy-two hours. That was too long, but we waited patiently. After the seventy-two hours, although I don't remember whether we quite waited all seventy-two hours, we sought each other. I had not at all thought that it was going to be a tough experience, but as we locked and rocked round and round without success, I sensed danger. It was as if our task was to pull down the moon with our bare hands. By morning I was tired, he was tired, and we had not reached anywhere. Our hearts were sore, our eyes were sore, our bodies were sore. We were consumed by a fire of desire and pain. The second night came and went just like the first one.

"In the middle of the third night, I offered to divorce and free the man I loved most. But you see, my wedding had been very dramatic, and the circumstances did not offer me many options. When my husband and I agreed to get married, none of our relatives supported us. They thought we were too young for marriage. He was 21 years old, and I was 20. But we felt ready. He was already out of school and working, and I was in my final year at university. We were in love, and we knew that we wanted to be husband and wife. When our parents refused, we did not argue with them. We had already made up our minds. His parents did not want to see me near their son, and my parents did not want him anywhere near their daughter.

"After one year, my boyfriend and I went ahead and secretly organised our wedding. We went to a monastery several kilometres away from home and stayed with monks for two days praying and getting to know each other more. We also used that time to arrange with a church near the monastery to conduct our wedding. On the third day, we went with our rings and were married. We stayed at the monastery still, in two different rooms, to fulfil the seventy-two-hour requirement. When the time was over, we proceeded to his home, where my real womanhood journey was yet to start.

"The major reason I offered to divorce him was not because we had failed to consummate our marriage but because he had insulted me. As he hit against the rock in the middle of the third night, he looked at me with daggers in his eyes and told me that I was a virgin not because I was a good girl but because other men had failed to penetrate me, just as he had failed. He was so angry about failing to consummate our marriage. I was so angry about the pain of his continuous rubbing and pressing, trying to force entry.

"I was also angry that after many years of purity on my part, the reward from my dear husband was to taunt me. That is when I offered to divorce him. I got up, picked up a jacket, stepped into my shoes, and staggered out of his house into the darkness outside. It was not easy leaving my marriage behind, but the physical pain I was suffering propelled me out of the house.

"See, this is how I walked home!"

Yemo gets up and walks the way she did the night her husband mocked her. She walks with bent knees and one leg cast here and the other leg cast there. I stare at her, my chin cupped in my left palm. I can imagine her pain spreading through my own body.

"I was in a sorry state, walking like a duck, careful not to open myself wide and cause further damage and careful not to rub against myself and cause more pain. One part of me told me to slump back on the bed and stay, but the other part was determined to leave my husband. Fortunately, our homes are less than one kilometre apart.

"When I got home, my mother was not amused to see me – for two reasons. One, I had eloped against her wishes, and so I had no right to leave the marriage I had gone into with eyes wide open. Two, she thought that I had started my marriage with a fighting spirit. She suspected that I was leaving because maybe I had discovered another girl in my husband's life. But that was very unfair. I really needed someone to talk to. Finding my mother at home had been such a relief because I knew that as a woman she would understand. You can imagine the disappointment I felt when she berated me instead!

"My mother did not even notice that I could hardly walk. But perhaps I shouldn't blame her. In my hurry to leave the house, I did not even notice that I had put a different type of shoe on each foot. One was brown and flat while the other was black and low-heeled. I noticed this later, as I sat down to talk to my mother. But I couldn't have cared less even if I had noticed. All I wanted was to get away from my husband's house.

"As I talked to my mother, I was shocked by her response.

"'You are not the first woman to be circumcised,' she said to me. 'Maybe you are a chincha,' she taunted further."

The word chincha sounds terrible on Yemo's tongue. It is said with anger and hatred, and that forces me to ask her to explain to me what it means.

"In my language, a chincha is a woman who is naturally frigid and runs away from men. Chinchas normally never get married because they cannot bear the touch of men. But how could my mother call me a chincha when she was fully aware of the role of the knife?"

As Yemo explained, I felt a surge of anger at women who do not protect women. I remembered a workshop I attended in 2003 that was held by Akina Mama Wa Africa, where one woman activist, Bisi Adeleye, declared that we all need to feel the pain of other women in order to do something about their situations. My anger spreads from mothers who take their daughters for 'circumcision', to women who are circumcisers, to the mothers-in-law who taunt their daughters-in-law and force them into 'circumcision' as if to avenge their own 'circumcision'.

"When she called me chincha, the tears I had held all along the way as I came home tumbled out of my eyes. When my mother saw the pain she had inflicted on my feelings she started counselling me. She told me that I should be patient and that with time it would be okay. I did not tell my mother that it was not me but my husband who required patience. I was determined not to go back to him because I did not see how anything was going to be okay.

"The following day, I was in bed when my sister came to tell me that I had a visitor. I told her to tell whoever it was to come inside. When she insisted that the person was in a hurry and could not come in, I guessed it was my husband. You see, in our customs, a husband is not supposed to enter his in-laws' house during such a time. I did not feel ready to see him, so I refused to come out. He was determined to see me, so he stayed at the gate and sent for me many more times, each time begging for my understanding. In the end, I went out and met him.

"When we talked, he apologised for his insult and said that he had spoken out of frustration. He begged and promised that he would be very patient with me and that together we would agree on what to do. He told me that if I agreed to go back to him, everything would be on my terms. I did not believe him, but – you will be surprised – I agreed to go back. I felt sympathetic, and also I decided I would give it one more try. But I knew what awaited me. Whatever plan we hatched, whatever strategy, we would have to be husband and wife.

"The day after his visit, I went back to his home. You see, being with my mother at home did not make things any easier for me. When I got there, I found my husband drinking arkie. There was a lot of it in our room. Arkie is a local brew in Ethiopia. I think his friends brought it to him to console him after I left. From the look of things, my husband had been drinking heavily since then.

"He offered me some arkie too. I took it and gulped it down as if I did not taste its bitterness. He was a little surprised when I asked for more. I drank more and more, and he drank with me. When I got drunk, I allowed him to touch me. He too was drunk. The more we drank, the more we loosened up, and eventually I became too drunk to stop what he was doing. But when he tore into me, I felt my whole body ripping open. I was too drunk to struggle, and he was drunk enough not to care about my screams, which shattered the night's silence. I am sure that his mother and his other family members heard me scream, but they did not come to my rescue.

"He raped me, and I bled profusely. I think I must have passed out for hours."

As Yemo describes the rape, my body recoils as if I am the one being assaulted. I grit my teeth and curse under my breath. God forbid.

"For more than ten days afterwards, I could not give in to his sexual advances. I was careful not to drink any more arkie. When I had agreed to drink it the first time, I was seeking the courage to be a wife to my husband. But now I had to be fully conscious. My husband begged and pleaded, but I could not agree. He told me that if I did not give in soon enough, my body would close up again and be even tighter. I cared, yes, but on the other hand, I did not care.

"After a while, his pleas melted me, and I gave in again. I had hoped that there would be less pain, but that was just wishful thinking because it was still very painful. With time, the pain became different. It shifted from the pain of tearing flesh to the pain of forced entry into a very narrow opening, the pain of heavy pressure. Even now, it still hurts. I still literally fight with my husband before I give in to his sexual demands. I understand that there are some women who ask their husbands for sex, but that is unheard-of in my life. On many occasions I create differences between us so that my husband and I are not on speaking terms. When we are at odds, he stays away from me, and that is my joy. However, he discovered my trick eventually, and now he doesn't always stay away.

"These days I use a special lubricant to soften myself up. But every time we have sex, there will always be blood, with or without Vaseline, and with or without force. Still, God has his own miracles. In all this mess, two children still found their way into our lives. In both cases, I delivered normally. I have no idea what happened, because after my deliveries I went back to my usual size, the size of fights over my marital obligations. I had hoped that normal delivery would do something for me. But I guess my problem is also about feelings. The knife takes all the feelings away.

"After my second child, I was fed up with the marriage institution, and I wanted out. I was sure that I wanted a divorce this time."

"But you are not a divorcee, or are you?" I ask Yemo, looking at the fancy wedding band on her finger.

"No, I am not divorced, my sister. You see, my husband and I love each other very much. It is so difficult for me to have sex with him, but I still love him. It's a dilemma the two of us were thrown into by the 'circumcision' that turned me into rock. When I told him of my intentions to divorce, he begged and pleaded, and I ended up staying. And I have decided to stay. But I will tell you the truth, my sister: I cry during every single sexual encounter with my husband. Of course it is only the four walls of our bedroom that know what goes on in there. Outside, we are a very happily married couple, handsome husband, cheerful wife, and two gorgeous children. Every day I ask God why he does not perform a miracle to return my senses to me and dissolve the rock that I am, but I know it will never happen. God can do it, can't he?"

Yemo looks at me expectantly. I have read in the Bible that Jesus performed miracles, but I do not remind her of that. I see her dilemma revealed in the contradictions of her statements. Her confusion cuts deep into my psyche. I sense the web of intrigue getting tighter round her neck. I want to tell Yemo that something can be done, but I am not sure what it is. Instead, we stretch out our arms and embrace. I feel part of her and part of her dilemma. And yes, something has to be done. A lot must be done.

Beverley Nambozo Nsengiyunva

My Sister learns her ABC

My sister learns her ABC.
She sings the rhymes
like laughter as it learns to fly.

I don't teach her about the V.
She will learn it herself
When her own V is opened
Like a door leading her to 'womanhood'.

Brenda Lubwama

My Mother's Wish

Letting my tears flow
was the only way I could refill my cup
that cup of life's joy
after long days of sorrow.
letting my heart flow out
was the only way to share pain
with the bloody girls
that littered the sacrificial floor
to make real women
Full beautiful wives
strong respected mothers

mother is with me
father insisted
she too does it
she wasn't sure
she's never been sure
not about hers
not about mine
she wanted to take me miles and miles away
but leaving her husband she couldn't dare
none would approve
the spirit of the land would follow

mother beckons me
she reads my face and I, hers
we decode hidden secrets
of stained matrimonial beds
of pleasures denied
of self denied
of womanhood denied

we hold hands and make a wish
we take an oath of allegiance
to protect what is ours
then we walk away and upset patriarchal order.

Bananuka Jocelyn Ekochu

Fly Beyond the Knife

Kapchorwa is a place of natural wonders that take your breath away. This beautiful green place in the eastern part of Uganda is the home of the Sabiny. The road to Kapchorwa town gently snakes its way up Mount Elgon between the giant rocks in their majestic postures, then meanders through the fertile land, continuing ever upward, as if the sky is its final destination.

Kapchorwa is the land where water flows out of rocks and mist hovers over the hills, forming a gigantic snow-white blanket. It is the place where sunshine and rain alternate so seamlessly that they have turned weathermen into liars. Kapchorwa sits proudly above the plains of Teso and Karamoja, beckoning visitors to come and partake of its abundant produce.

In a remote village in Kwoti Parish, Kaptanya Sub-county, an African beauty was born twenty-five years ago. Her name is Bena. She is the first of seven children, four girls and three boys, born to poor, conservative parents who were a little enlightened, and who therefore tried hard to keep Bena and her siblings in school.

"But girls and boys were always treated differently," Bena says, recalling her childhood. "We would all go to work in the shamba, but when we finished, the girls were made to carry the hoes and the food. When we got home, we had to go and fetch water from the well, collect firewood, and prepare food for the family while the boys rested. This was the accepted order of things. It did not matter that men are considered the stronger sex. Women had to do the hard work."

At the age of six, Bena started school. She loved school. School was a place where she could read, write, and sing ABC. At school, she could run and shout without being reminded that as a girl she was expected to keep her voice low. At school, she was allowed to be a child. Back home, she behaved herself and dreamt of the following day, when she would go to school again. Weekends were unbearably long for her, having to stay home two full days. She never understood why there should be holidays at all. As far as she was concerned, there was no need to rest -- one does not need to rest from fun. Once in a while, some children were caned for being naughty, but all in all, school was fun.

When Bena was fourteen, in Senior Two, her parents could no longer afford school fees for all the children, so Bena had to drop out. Her dreams were effectively put on hold. She had wanted to study up to university, after which she would get a good job. But it was not to be. Stopping school was a hard blow to her, but there was nothing she could do about it. Her parents could not afford school fees any longer, and that was that.

"It was very hard for me to accept at first, but eventually I got used to it," she says.

Watching her calmly narrating her story, admiring her genuine African beauty, with the kind of skin, untouched by make-up, that a model would kill for, I wonder what direction Bena's life might have taken if she had been born in a liberated society, under better circumstances.

As soon as Bena left school, she was automatically available for marriage, whether she was willing or not. She could not make her own decisions in such matters. She was only a girl. And for most Sabiny, early marriage was the norm.

One day in 1998, shortly after Bena had dropped out of school, the unthinkable happened to her. On her way from town, as she approached her home, she had a strange feeling that something was wrong. She ignored it, but suddenly something moved in the bush, and just as suddenly a group of young men sprang out, startling her. What was all this about?

Bena didn't know what they wanted, so she tried to walk past them. However, one of them grabbed her hand, hurting her in the process. She tried to free herself, but she was no match for the man. Suddenly she stopped struggling and started trembling as the realisation hit her: they were either going to rape her or force her into marriage!

"Please let me go," she pleaded. "My father will beat me if I'm not home soon."

"You are not going anywhere," one of them responded. "Your father has failed to pay your school fees, and as you are old enough, I'm taking you to be my wife."

"No! I don't want to get married. My father will find the money to send me back to school. Please let me go!"

"You should be happy that I'm going to be your husband. A girl who is not circumcised cannot find a husband. I'm helping you. Who else would want you?" he taunted.

"But I don't want to be married," she insisted.

"And I do want to marry you," he replied.

All this time the man's friends had said nothing. Then one of them cleared his throat and said, "We are not going to waste any more time with you. You either go with your husband or we will kill you," he said. He casually fondled the panga he was carrying.

Bena was finally taken away against her will. Within a matter of minutes, her life had been determined for her. It did not matter that she did not consent to it, nor did the fact that she was still a minor protect her. This was a moment she would always remember.

They took her to a place near the border with Kenya, where she stayed with her captor-turned-husband for two months. The man seemed to adore her. He was always at her side and did everything possible to please her. By the end of the time, Bena had not only accepted her fate but had also developed feelings for him. She had grown to love the man who had kidnapped her and forcibly made her his wife. After the two months, the man took her to his home back in Kapchorwa.

"All this time I thought I was his only wife. But when we went to his home I found that he was already married." Bena recounts her first disappointment in the man she had grown to love. He had concealed his marital status from her, and this knowledge did not go down well.

"When I asked him, he told me that the reason he had married me was because he did not like a circumcised woman. His first wife was circumcised, and he was not satisfied with her sexually. He said that I would always be his favourite wife."

At fourteen, a girl will believe anything she is told by the man she thinks she loves. During the time she spent alone with him, she actually counted herself lucky to have caught his eye. So she accepted his explanation and believed his promise. Life was almost perfect, but there was a problem.

"My mother-in-law hated me. I was not allowed to fetch water before circumcised women at the well, nor could I climb into a granary to get millet, or handle cow dung, either to clean the kraal or to smear the floor of my hut. Nobody listened to me, and I could not make any decision, even if it concerned me," she says, almost in tears.

"Who allowed that girl to draw water before we did?" someone would ask, if a group of women happened to find her at the communal well. They called her a girl because she was not circumcised and was therefore not a real woman. They would throw her jerry can aside, pouring out the water she had drawn. She was expected to wait for them all to get water before she could even approach the well.

"Don't touch the cow dung."

"You can't climb into the granary."

"Don't pass behind me, you are not circumcised."

"Shut up, girl. You are not circumcised."

Bena was being punished because her parents had resisted pressure to have her and her sisters subjected to female genital mutilation, an age-old practice among the Sabiny. In earlier times, female 'circumcision' had been compulsory, and those who resisted it were cut by force. However, by the time Bena grew up it had been outlawed by the District Council, and only those who chose it would go for it. Still, the perpetrators of this harmful and painful practice used intimidation to ensure that it did not die out.

With all the intimidation that she experienced, Bena found herself wondering why she should not have herself circumcised and have some peace in her home.

"After all, it would not kill me. There would be pain, but I would earn respect by becoming a full woman," she reasoned.

But her husband did not want her to go through with it. "He told me that he had married me because he wanted a complete woman, one who had all her body parts intact. He did not want a circumcised woman."

His preference, however, did not stop the intimidation and harassment that she was going through. Her in-laws were merciless, and she did not have any friends in the community. She was treated as an outcast, or someone who had a highly contagious disease. She was only able to go on with her life because she had the full support of her husband. He had said, after all, that she would remain his favourite wife because she was not circumcised. She could therefore try to ignore all the others and go on with her life. Then the babies started coming.

"I was very happy when I had my first child, but I noticed that my husband was not. The baby was a girl. I did not mind, but I hoped the next child would be a boy and then my husband would be happy. To tell the truth, I very much wanted the next one to be a boy because my co-wife had both boys and girls," she recounts.

The taunting by her in-laws and other villagers worsened after the birth of her daughter. Bena also noticed that her husband was not as protective of her as before. Before, he would tell his relatives that she was his wife and he was not bothered by her uncircumcised state. But now he kept quiet or just walked away and left her to bear the insults alone.

When the second child arrived, she realised why her husband was no longer supportive. "Another girl?," he exclaimed with intense anger. But Bena now understood that she was being blamed for producing only girls. She knew that boys were the preferred sex among the Sabiny, but she had not understood the magnitude of the problem.

"I knew as a man he wanted to have a boy, but I thought it was unfair of him to blame me for not producing one. I'm not God, am I?"

But her husband had no intention of being reasonable. Bena was the one carrying the babies, and therefore she was to blame for not giving him a son. Couldn't she follow his first wife's example?

"He started comparing me to his other wife. He would outline her good points and compare them with what he said were my bad points. I was no longer his favourite wife but someone useless, who had brought him nothing but shame. I did not know what to do, and I wondered what made a baby girl such a shameful object." Bena asked herself the question that any rational human being would ask.

The proverbial straw that broke the camel's back was the third child – another girl. This time Bena's husband did not mince words. "If I had known that you were going to produce only girls, I wouldn't have married you," he raged.

"But...but...," she stammered in her confusion. Why couldn't he understand that she did not decide the sex of her children?

"Shut up, you uncircumcised woman. Who gave you permission to say anything?"

Was this the husband who supposedly married her because she

was not circumcised? What could Bena do? Who could reason with her husband? Since she was an uncircumcised woman, her husband had never paid any bride price to her parents. She was therefore hesitant to go home and consult her mother. She had no friend to talk to since she was shunned by almost everybody.

One evening Bena's husband came home from his usual drinking spree. He had started avoiding her and seemed to make sure he had nothing to do with her, but now he sat down next to her, something he had stopped doing. Bena's heart skipped a beat.

"I was happy when he sat with me. I thought someone had talked to him and he was beginning to see reason."

He asked for food, which she hurried to bring. She would do anything to please him. He had come back to her, and that was what mattered. Maybe God would remember her and her next child would be a boy. How happy she would be!

"He ate in silence, and I thought he was tired. I did not want to say anything in case I said something that would annoy him."

After his meal, he angrily pushed the plate away. Bena's heart sank. The eagerness with which she had received him home evaporated in the space of a second. How this hurt her! How she wished she could have her loving husband back!

"I knew then that he had not come in peace. He was angry about something. I didn't know what it was, but I was scared. After a short time he cleared his throat and said, 'I've been informed that if you were circumcised you would change from having girls and start having boys. I think you should do it.'

"'But you said you didn't want a circumcised woman,' I dared remind him.

"'Now I'm saying I want you to get circumcised and start doing your duty of giving me boys,' he retorted. I didn't know what to say, so I kept quiet. But I knew that he was wrong."

Although Bena knew there was no truth in what her husband was saying, she still nursed thoughts of being circumcised, if only to be accepted in society as a full Sabiny woman. But she also remembered that her husband had said he had married her because she was not circumcised. Would he still want her if she did it? She was confused.

"Then I remembered that his first wife was circumcised and he had gone back to her. If that's what he wanted, then I would get circumcised, and hopefully then he would come back to me. I started praying for a baby boy because I knew that was the problem. If God gave me a baby boy, my husband would be happy and we would go on as before. Society would also accept me, and I would not have to bear the insults that were heaped on me on a daily basis," she says, the look in her eyes seeking understanding. "I really didn't want to go back home to my parents. I loved my husband, and I thought that if getting circumcised was the only way to save my marriage, I would do it."

Bena made up her mind to be circumcised. She would go home to arrange her 'circumcision'. Her parents would then receive the bride price they had missed and everybody would be happy.

"When I got home, my parents were not happy because they never wanted us to be cut in the first place. But they said that if that was what my husband wanted, then I should go ahead with it."

In the year 2002, Bena went through the most painful and humiliating experience of her life. "They made me dance throughout the night in the cold. People did all sorts of things to provoke and humiliate me. Someone could, for example, spit in his hands and order me to lick the spittle, and I had to oblige. Others would pour water on the ground and tell us to sit or roll in the mud," she says, the expression on her face showing the disgust she felt. During the 'circumcision' preparation period, girls are expected to tolerate all sorts of nonsense. Bena was ready to endure it all bravely in an attempt to save her marriage. She looked forward to a normal life with her children and their father.

At dawn, the actual 'circumcision' was done. "But the pain was unbearable, and I bled a lot. It is not even comparable to childbirth. It was something worse than I had ever experienced before or imagined, something that I wouldn't want another person to go through."

Nothing was done to relieve the pain, and nothing at all to treat the wound. It was understood that real women did not need any medication. They were instructed to look after their wounds using their own urine.

"We were told to press our thighs together every time we needed to pass urine. Then we would let it run through the wound. It was so painful that we needed something to hold on to. You had to hug a tree or a pole until the pain subsided, which took a long time. We were expected not to cry out or complain," she says, her face reflecting the pain she remembered from years before, the kind of pain that never goes away. The physical pain may go, but the mental anguish lingers, the trauma remains always at the back of the mind.

She was taken to her parents' home to recover. Nobody thought of taking her to hospital. It was simply unheard-of to take a circumcised girl to a doctor. Two weeks passed before she could walk properly again. Eventually the wound healed and she could do some simple chores. But her husband never appeared. Not at the 'circumcision' place, not at her parents' home.

"We waited for him, but he did not come. He was supposed to pay the surgeon and the mentors. He was also supposed to bring me food, but he never did."

There is a Luganda saying, 'Nanyini mufu y'akwat'awawunya,' meaning that the individual closest to a dead person is the one who handles the smelly part. This was the case with Bena and her parents. In the first place, they did not support her undergoing the knife, yet they were the ones handed the bill for the mutilation of their daughter.

Shortly after the 'circumcision', Bena's daughters were brought to her. She was happy to see them. She had missed them a lot. They had a happy reunion until she was told that they were not expected back home. Their father, Bena's husband, did not want them anymore. Bena was devastated. But why doesn't he want them back? she asked herself. Hadn't she followed his orders? Wasn't she circumcised, as he said he wanted?

At the back of her mind, Bena knew that the 'circumcision' had been her husband's ruse to get rid of her. He had sent her to her parents with no intention of picking her up. Now he had sent away her daughters too, to make sure that she had no excuse for going back.

"My husband no longer wanted me, and he was now rejecting his own children," she says, her voice full of grief.

The family did not expect the man to abandon his wife and children in such a manner, so they kept trying to talk to him. But he avoided them. They sent other people to talk to him. Why was he rejecting his wife?

"We tried to reach him through his friends and relatives, but he told them that he did not want a circumcised woman."

"How could he say that? He never sent away his other wife, who is circumcised."

This was confusing, seeing that he was the one who had insisted on the 'circumcision' in the first place. It slowly dawned on Bena that she had been tricked into accepting a dreadful practice just so that she could be got rid of. Her husband had never intended to take her back. She saw he was a chameleon in human skin.

Bena grew more and more depressed. Life seemed unbearably cruel. First of all, she had been forced out of school because her parents didn't have the money for her fees, then she was forced into marriage, and because she seemed unable to produce boys, she had been forced into 'circumcision'. Now she had been abandoned, with three young children to care for.

In the meantime, Bena's father wanted her husband to pay the bride price for his daughter. When a Sabiny man marries his first wife, the bride price will be paid by his father. But because Bena was a second wife, her husband was supposed to pay the bride price himself. A second wife is expected to work hard for the payment. Then her husband would take what she has worked for to his in-laws. Because Bena was not circumcised when she was abducted, her bride price was not considered a priority. But now things had changed: she was a circumcised woman, and her father wanted what was due to him.

However, Bena's husband no longer wanted her. He had no intention of paying the bride price. To make matters worse, Bena's parents, with their limited resources, now had to feed their three granddaughters too. Something needed to be done about the situation. Where was the law?

In 2004, Bena's parents took her husband to court, with the help of the Women Lawyers Federation (FIDA). They wanted him to be charged with kidnapping their daughter, forcing her into an early marriage and 'circumcision' against her will, and then abandoning his children. They also wanted him to pay her bride price.

The magistrate summoned the husband. "Do you know this woman?" he asked him.

"Yes, I know her."

"Is she your wife?"

"Yes."

"Why have you abandoned her?"

"My friends were laughing at me for staying with a woman who could only give me girls. They said that when I died, with no sons to protect her she would be everyone's property."

"Why did you force her to be circumcised?"

"Because I was told that if she got circumcised she would produce boys."

"What about the children?"

"They are also mine."

"Why have you abandoned them?"

"I was told that when I died they would not be called mine."

For some reason, the kidnapping and forced marriage, which was actually rape, was not mentioned. The magistrate ordered Bena's husband to pay a minimum of 30,500 Uganda shillings (about $15) per child per month as child support. He said he would, but in fact he had no intention of complying.

"Up to now he has never paid a single shilling," Bena laments.

Then, typically, one day he decided he wanted Bena back. "But you said you didn't want a circumcised woman," she protested.

"Now I want you to come home," he insisted in an arrogant tone. He was a man, and she must do his bidding. The decision as to whether she would go with him or stay at home with her parents was his to make. She had no say in how things would go. After all, she was only a woman.

But Bena had had enough. The time she had spent at home with her parents had given her a chance to look back at her life, the way it had gone since she got married. "I remembered all the suffering I went through and realised that it would not change," she says. "The man wanted a boy, and I wasn't sure I would give him one. Moreover, I did not desire him or any man anymore. You see, before 'circumcision', I really desired him and enjoyed sex with him. But afterwards I realised that all the sexual feelings in me had died." Bena did the unthinkable -- she refused to go back to her husband.

Sadly, Bena has been harbouring hopes of having her womanhood restored. "They told us that there is a place in Kampala where they can repair mutilated private parts. But I understand it is very expensive. I don't think I can afford it."

It breaks my heart to have to dash her hopes and tell her that nothing can be done for her currently. Maybe in the future, when science advances to that level, the victims of FGM may have some hope. But she has to be told the truth, otherwise someone may take advantage of her desperate situation and cheat her and other unsuspecting victims out of their meagre resources. Now her main interest is in raising her daughters and protecting them from FGM.

Bena is one of the fortunate few. In Kapchorwa, once a girl has been married, she is not expected back in her parents' home except as a visitor. She loses her place in the home of her birth and will more often than not be forced back to her husband's place. It doesn't matter what she is going through, she has to return to him. Luckily, Bena was accepted back by her parents, though she needed to contribute to the upkeep of her family.

"I could not sit and watch my mother break her back on our behalf. So I thought of going to 'government lodge.'"

"Government lodge" is a slum in Kapchorwa town where all sorts of disreputable practices go on. Prostitution is rife, with girls as young as thirteen taking the lead. Young boys shack up with sugar mommies who initiate them into sex. Men abandon their families and waste their money in this place. The locals believe that the name "government lodge" arose from the fact that numerous government officials frequent the place. The story goes that one white man who was looking for accommodation and requested to be taken to "government lodge," thinking that it was a respectable government hostel, was taken to the slum instead.

But what would Bena do in this place, since she no longer wanted to have sex with anyone?

"I was determined to make money. I wasn't going into it for the pleasure of sex. I was only too willing to suffer for my children. I wanted to raise enough money to start a small business. Then I would quit prostitution."

Innocently, Bena confided in her mother and one of her brothers.

"I thought they would be relieved because I would be bringing in money to help run the home, but I was mistaken."

Bena's mother and brother made it clear that if she went ahead with her plan, they would not want anything to do with her. She would cease to exist for them, and they would consider her dead. Her mother assured her that the family would continue sharing the little they had with her, that whatever was available belonged to them all.

But Bena did not want to sit and do nothing with her life and her future. She decided to go back to school. This was not easy. Her brother had stopped in Senior Six because there had been no money for him to continue. Her three sisters had stopped in Primary Seven and had been unable to go any further. Where was she going to get the school fees? Bena felt desperate.

"My mother called us all together for a meeting one day to consider my problem and come up with a solution. At the meeting, it was decided that we would sell a cow to pay for the first term."

So, at the beginning of 2008, Bena joined Kapchorwa Parents Secondary School, in Senior Two. At the moment her brothers are engaged in odd jobs, and they contribute to her tuition. But of course she does not know how long that will last.

"I don't know if I will make it to Senior Four. There is simply no money. But I'm determined to continue with my education," she vows. "They took my womanhood away, but I'm still alive. I will work hard. I will be someone one day. I am determined to live beyond the knife."

So what will happen to Bena's sisters? They are out of school, and they are as vulnerable as she was when she dropped out.

"I have strongly advised them not to get circumcised. I tell them to learn from me. Many people have come up now to fight the practice, and since it is now illegal to force someone to do it, women can actually avoid it. But Kapchorwa is Kapchorwa. All the girls need to be informed, advised, and protected."

I look at Bena, still fascinated by her beauty. I am very glad that she is determined to study and to fly beyond the knife.

Bena is one of the few women who have come out openly to denounce the practice in Kapchorwa. She tells her story readily, hoping to sensitise young girls and save them from the knife. She is collaborating with REACH, a Kapchorwa programme whose aim is to enhance reproductive health, prevent HIV/AIDS and gender-based violence, and care for widows and orphans and victims of FGM.

But the question is, must one lose one's womanhood in order to understand how deadly the practice is?

Alal Sopphie Brenda

In Kapchorwa

Beside us
On this scenic evening
The banana leaves are split into ribbons
Swaying in the breeze.
People too seem to be clothed in ribbons.

Whole hills seem etched with human life,
indelible against the shifting clouds,
the rocky hillsides, ants on safari, sharp eyed eagles
on silent wings
huts painted with human voices.
Women, with lips knowingly pursed
Pass us by.

Little girls we pass by
One of them may be next.
To have ribbons,
sliced from the pursed lips between her legs
next rite season.

Arlen Atutambira

A Little Time

Give me a little time
to catch my breath
a little time
to rub the twinge around my scar
to unlearn my stain
to meditate on my pain.
a little time
to live my engrave
I am not
Little anymore

Mocked by Fate

"The man with the keys will be here soon." The receptionist in the REACH offices put her phone back in her bag. I had come to REACH to meet some of the brave women of Kapchorwa. These few minutes gave me a chance to enjoy the unique beauty of this land of contradictions.

Surrounding the town lay the expanse of lush green vegetation covering the steep slopes of the hills beyond. The thick shrubbery and trees disappeared into deep gorges only to emerge again on the other side, imposing and magnificent. In some places, the woodland appeared to vanish suddenly over the horizon. The view was so picturesque that its magical beauty left me spellbound.

It was an unusual experience to be so close to nature, seemingly intact and undisturbed by modern changes and the customs of its inhabitants. Looking at it all – the woodland that covered the steep slopes of ancient Mount Elgon, the leisurely pace of the town – made me wonder if there was an unspoken order that no one should awaken the giant whose mighty bones protruded to form the mountain's awe-inspiring rocks, and through whose mouth sprang the dazzling Sipi Falls.

Kapchorwa, here I come to unearth the well-kept secrets that cut the beauty out of your daughters and make your sons endure your harsh brutality! Your serenity deceives girls with promises of making them women, yet you rob them of their womanhood. I judge you, Kapchorwa! My thoughts flew over the hills and down through the valleys and resonated back to me as I eagerly awaited the women I was to meet that day.

In determined silence, Kapchorwa enveloped us in its cold embrace as the sun winked from behind the clouds. It struggled to make its way out to offer its anticipated radiance. We pulled our sweaters closer to our bodies to ward off the chill.

I looked at my watch a little impatiently. I did not want to lose precious time. I had met some of the women the day before, and they had said they would come back this morning. A moment later, I saw them walking toward us up the slope. When they joined us on the veranda, they greeted us in Kupsabiny – the language spoken by the Sabiny – and the translator gave me the words to respond. We conversed a little with the help of the translator.

Cherop, my interviewee, was of medium height, of slight build, and with a light-brown complexion. From her manner of dress and appearance I could tell she was someone who had always had to struggle to make whatever little progress she did. There was a kind of tired look about her, and something close to disgust on her small, round face.

She was quite good-looking, but it was obvious that she was not well cared for, just like most peasants in Uganda. She could very well have done with a new khanga wrapper. The one she wore around her shoulders had obviously seen better days. Her face showed pleasure as she came nearer and, like most of her people, she had a lovely smile that exposed a set of pure white teeth.

"I was born in 1962 in a village called Tuban," she started her story. "My home was poor. We were four girls and three boys in our family. Despite our severe poverty, I was able to attend Tuban Primary School and managed to complete Primary Seven. It did not matter whether I qualified to go to secondary school or not because there was no money, anyway, to pay for me to continue with school. So my education ended there.

"After I left school my routine changed. I got myself into the village work that everyone did, fetching water and digging in the shamba. Time passed quickly, and soon it was another even year, a year for 'circumcision'. That was an exciting time. The dancing started early in August, and I did not have any reason not to join in. For me it was good enough to know that I would soon change from a child into a respected woman.

"In 1980 I was a petite eighteen-year-old. I was light-footed and known for my agility as a dancer. I was the leader of my group in many songs.

"During that year's 'circumcision' season I stood out for being unafraid of the circumciser's knife. My mother had taken time to explain that 'circumcision' was the fate of a woman, like giving birth, and I had to take it as a natural step in my life.

"When it was my turn on the day of the knife, I closed my eyes and clenched my teeth as the sharp blade cut through my flesh. I cannot lie and say I was not shocked – I was, and given a chance I would have screamed my lungs out. But I did not make a sound, because that pain was the fate of a woman and I wanted to be a woman. During our preparations, our mentor had explained that it was a cowardly act to squirm or show fear or make any sound that suggested feelings of pain during 'circumcision'. She had told us that becoming a woman had a price and that it required us to be brave. And we, eager and wide-eyed as we were, ready to leave childhood with all its innocence, hung on to her every word.

"So after the cut I tried to spring up and validate people's expectations of me, but my head reeled and I could only get up slowly. I saw the circumciser wipe the blood off the knife as she put it quickly back into her pouch, ready for the next candidate. I could not bear the sight, and that gave me the impetus to move faster. Despite the biting pain, I swiftly moved away to create space for the next girl.

"I got married four years after my 'circumcision'. I was 22 years old. Since I was circumcised, according to our beliefs I was a woman. I was no longer in school, so I should have been ready for the next step. Strangely enough, I did not feel ready for marriage."

I listened to Cherop's steady and poignant voice.

"Truthfully, if I had had my way, I would not have got married, but it was different then. Back then, a girl did not have a say about anything in her life. So my husband was chosen for me, and I had no choice but to marry him at that time.

"It was actually my father who chose this man for me. It was fine for a father to do that. I did not know the man very well. I knew him only casually because he was from our village. Nobody asked me if I liked him or not. My father just called me one morning and told me that I was going to be married to him. Although my mother was present, she never said anything to contradict my father. So he broke the news. It was final, he had expressed his wish, and nobody could change it.

"According to our customs, I was now a proper woman, circumcised and married to a man that my family had chosen, and this ought to have been the beginning of a happy life, but the formula did not work very well for us.

"It was all wrong, very wrong, right from the beginning. It was quite unusual for that sort of thing to happen in marriages in those days. But the truth is, we were totally unsuited for each other. As a result it turned out that neither of us was ready for the responsibilities of marriage. Neither of us knew which direction to take to solve our problems. We did not understand each other, and we did not even try to work at understanding each other. So we argued a lot and disagreed on many things. I did not like his friends, for example, because of the way they seemed to control him. Another thing that caused numerous quarrels between us was money. We were very poor, both of us coming from similarly poor families. It was strange, but at times I imagined that I could have been better off marrying a man who had other women but did not quarrel with me about the way I used things, or who could provide a little better for our children.

"We were poor and I knew it, but he was kind of selfish in his priorities. I would tell him so, something that he did not like at all. Then there were his friends, but to make it worse we had no one in either family who could give us help of any kind, such as good advice or even a goat or a chicken to sell, or anything to alleviate our situation. The extended family members were all poor too and of no use to us. We were unfortunate because most families here have many people who can help, but we did not. So we would struggle on our own for everything, including food, and when the children came along, it just got worse.

"We would probably have lived with our problems, which were not really extraordinary, if it had not been for an even bigger problem. It was bad, because when my husband introduced that problem, our quarrels became even more frequent and virulent, and then the worst happened. That was when he started staying away.

"You see, one day he came and told me that his friends had told him that circumcised women were not good. I am being decent here, but he would use the most obscene words, just to embarrass me, perhaps so that I would not answer him. His strategy worked because what he said stunned me for quite some time. I just listened to him in silence. I waited for his ranting to end, but it did not. So I finally had to stand up for myself and tell him what was on my mind. First of all, I reminded him that he was a Sabiny and that Sabiny men married Sabiny women who were circumcised. Then I reminded him of all our customs and traditions and beliefs. I also reminded him that when we were growing up we were always told that Sabinys never left their land – even after they were educated they always came back home to work and live, and married here.

"He listened, and for a time I thought that he was going to change his mind. How silly of me to even have thought of such a thing! He would seem to understand, but then by evening he would go away again. I asked him where he spent so much of his time, and that would set off a quarrel. Once a quarrel started, I knew what would come next. Bedroom affairs would certainly come up, as well as his favourite topic of comparing circumcised to uncircumcised women. This would not help us at all, and things would just go from bad to worse.

"With time I realised that he was not just repeating what his friends were telling him but that he was actually sleeping with other women, and in the process he had discovered what everyone knew but never talked about – that uncircumcised women were sexually more satisfying.

"Finally I asked him what he wanted me to do. I told him this was our culture, respected and upheld for generations.

"'What do you want me to do?' I cried out one time, but he did not give me any answer. I told him I could not remake myself. I had been cut, and that was how I would remain for the rest of my life. I told him over and over again that in our culture a girl had to be cut in order for her to become a woman.

"I remember one time asking him whether his mother would have respected me if I had not been circumcised, but he gave no answer. He ignored such questions or just became rude enough to kill the conversation. I told him I was going to talk to his mother, and he replied that his mother had nothing to do with it. He had become an expert in vulgar language because he knew I hated it, and some of the expressions he used were so shocking that I wondered where he had learnt them.

"Things got steadily worse. He started really mistreating me. He stopped caring for anything at home, as if he were not part of us anymore. We had two girls and one boy. When he started going away openly and not coming home for days, I knew I had lost him. But I did not go back to my parents. I stayed on in his home, and I still live there, but he does not stay there anymore. He lives somewhere else. He has a Mugisu wife from the neighbouring district of Mbale, where they do not circumcise women."

"Tell me what you felt when you realised that he had left you because you were circumcised when the act was specifically done to initiate you into womanhood," I asked her. "Did you see it as a great cultural deception?"

"It was a time of great confusion for me. I felt lost and deliberately misled. I asked myself a lot of questions, but I had no answers. If what my husband was claiming was true, why did our culture condone the 'circumcision' of women? One could not become a woman unless she was cut, period. Now that I was a proper woman and married, the man was saying something else, so who was fooling whom?

"I remember going to my mother to talk to her about it, but she did not have an answer. Of course she knew of some of the side-effects of 'circumcision', but surprisingly she had never told me about them. She told me that day that she knew two women whose private parts had closed up completely because of the way they were told to keep the legs tightly together while the 'circumcision' wound healed. She said that these women were too embarrassed to talk about their problem, and it was other people who whispered about them behind their backs. Both women avoided getting married.

"I could not find anybody to explain why our people were bent on damaging women through cutting them, and what people like us could do. So I stopped trying to find answers and resigned myself to just getting my children through school. Thank God, they are big now, although my daughter had to drop out of school in Senior One due to lack of school fees. She soon got married, at sixteen years of age. I know this was too early for her, but we did not have a choice in the matter since she could not just stay at home without attending school and without a job."

"But how did you manage when your husband left? How did you sustain the family?" I asked with interest.

"It was hard after he left because, in spite of our misunderstandings, he at least gave me help once in a while. But now he cut us off completely. To sustain the children and myself I brewed local beer for sale. In that way I have been getting some money to keep me going, but of course it is not enough. My son is still in school, for which I thank God. Right now he is preparing to sit for his O-level exams this November (2008). His father does not give us any help, so I take full responsibility for everything."

"I understand that you were also a mentor for the 'circumcision' candidates." I had heard that those involved in the 'circumcision' business earned money from it.

"No, I was not a mentor, but I was a circumciser's assistant," she corrected. "I was the person who moves with the circumciser and holds some of her tools to enable her to move faster. I would say that I got into the work almost by accident. It was not in my lineage or anything like that, but I had a neighbour who was a circumciser. One day she approached me and asked me to be her assistant. I accepted eagerly because it was going to help me earn a little more money for the children. At the time, I was not thinking about anything else. I did not connect it with my own problems. All I could think about was that I had been abandoned by my husband and I needed an income to help me raise my children. Moreover, even if I had refused, it would not have stopped this circumciser from doing her work. She would have looked for another willing person, so it would not have made any difference at all.

"It took me a long time to actually believe that it was the genital mutilation that had destroyed my marriage. In my heart I was blaming my husband for everything. Of course, I still know that he was wrong to leave me and to forget his children as well."

The bitterness in her voice was unmistakable.

"Even if he had chosen just to look after the children, I would still be angry with him because he knew I was circumcised when we got married. I did not fully believe him when he kept singing the difference between circumcised and uncircumcised women. I had my doubts. He is a man, and they always make up reasons for leaving. Secondly, at that time nobody talked about the problems resulting from FGM, like they are doing now. We had been socialised to love our culture and traditions, and all I could think about at that time was that my husband was just looking for an excuse to desert me.

"Only recently did I begin hearing people discussing the problems that come from 'circumcision'. At the time my husband and I were having our problems, I had never heard of anybody opposing the practice. Even if I had heard such talk, I would have thought them crazy because female 'circumcision' is such an essential part of our culture that for me to think that it could be stopped was not possible then.

"When the circumciser approached me to be her assistant, I did not connect all that had happened to me to the work I was asked to do. I was only relieved to be able to earn something to help the family.

"As I told you, the circumciser was my neighbour, and she knew all about me. Besides, I had this reputation of being very quick and hard-working. A circumciser needs to work fast, and this one knew me well and that I could manage it. Being a small-sized person has always been an advantage for me when speed is required. When the circumciser asked me to work with her, I did not know what to do, but she offered to train me. After she taught me what to do, I started moving with her. Besides, in our culture, circumcisers are respected because it is known that they are chosen by the spirits. And I knew how this particular one was chosen. We knew each other well.

"My duty was to hold the millet flour. Millet flour is part of the equipment used in the 'circumcision' ritual. It is not medicinal or anything like that. It is poured on the genitals to make them sticky and enable the circumciser to grip them firmly and make the cut. Being her assistant meant that I would always move with her, carrying the calabash of flour, as she went from place to place during the 'circumcision' season, wherever her services were contracted.

"So I assisted in cutting these innocent girls without ever realising the negative impact it was going to have on their lives. For me it was a job like any other, and I was totally ignorant of its bad effects.

"Moreover, I thought I was doing them a favour, helping them to accomplish what those before them had always done. It was the life, the fate of every Sabiny woman. I had gone through it myself. Maybe it would bring them better things than I had received. I saw the cutting was tough for them, too, but I could not save them from their fate. Besides, I needed the money to care for my children.

"I finally stopped assisting the circumciser in 2004. That was when I began hearing people on the radio campaigning against the cutting of girls. It did not take a lot of explanation for me, and I didn't need convincing. The minute I heard what they were saying, I knew that was what was needed. In addition, from my work with the circumciser, I could see that the number of girls being circumcised was getting smaller and smaller because of those campaigns against the practice. So I decided to heed the calls. I had begun to understand the negative effects of FGM and how dangerous it was to women.

"As for my marriage, I know now that my husband was probably right to look for a woman who was whole, but I still blame him for his neglect. I also still believe that as a person who knew the culture, he should have been able to stick with me. We both belong to the same culture, and he should have been able to understand.

"Now I am very happy that there are people out there trying to stop the practice. I am glad that a new era has started. My daughter married young, but she is not circumcised, and I know that nobody can force her into it. In the future, I would be happy to know that this practice has been stopped completely."

"Do you know that a law is being drafted to make this practice a criminal offence?" I asked her.

"No, I do not," she said, "but I know there are organisations that de-campaign the practice and this has helped us to protect our daughters. The circumcisers who believe that they have no control over their destiny to become circumcisers need to find alternative ways to earn a living. Maybe they should go to church, because I have seen that when people go to church they become better."

"Are churches very active here in Kapchorwa? The Christian church has been in Uganda for more than 100 years. How come they have not been able to eliminate such beliefs?"

"The church has not been very effective, but I have noticed that more and more people are going to church these days -- more than they used to. So I think they have seen something there. I do not go to church so much myself, but I have begun going once in a while, when time allows. The problem is that my beer business is time-consuming. You see, since 2004, when I stopped working with the circumciser, my only income comes from brewing beer. REACH has promised us some financial assistance, and so there is some hope for us to sustain ourselves, and our families."

I shook Cherop's hand and thanked her for agreeing to talk to me. She smiled and held my hand firmly, as if to reassure me that all would be well with her. And later, as I left Kapchorwa, I knew that the deception was coming to an end, and that the magnificent beauty of this place would at last be reflected in the lives of its people.

Wudalat Gedamu (Ethiopia)

SAY 'NO"
(Translated from Amharic)

You see my sister,
It was so terrible ... I know
To disclose one's sorrow ... yes,
It was boldness ... to say the truth
To undo the secret ... of womanhood
Fearing a taboo ... discuss misery
No one tried ... sharing the worry
To expose the issue ... to tell the story.

What a pity?
Committed evil ... to the voiceless
It was the period ... to engrave
My cry is deep ... to avenge the mess
Mental abuse ... body abuse
Unless one dared ... to be out cast
No one shall say 'NO' ... violate history?
There was no place ... the door to unshut
No breathing ... bleeding the heart
Better die woman ... her alienation

It was uncommon ... even impossible
To tell the narrative ... of this taboo
But alas
Protest arose ... It's another day today
It's my right ... possible to say.
You can say, NO ... to deeds of the devil
You must say no ... disclose the evil
Time to fight ... the bedeviled weevil

Hilda Twongyeirwe

Threshold

I am fifteen
The moon giggles shyly and caresses the skies
Sippi Falls cascades in a wave of excitement.
I waltz with the falls downstream
A tinge of warmth engulfs me
My feet rub …
My future

The village awakes
It is the rite season
The search …
She descends with a knife
I grip my tears and wash her thirst
She scoops.

I shift. …
The soothing sounds of Sippi Falls stand at a distance
Muffled by a stiffness … a pain
A lonely pain
My womanhood is robbed
I have become a woman …
My future

Cathy Anite

Saina's Story

Cherotich Saina was a seventy-year-old illiterate Muslim woman who had lost her husband and her two children in 1993. Her husband had been a lot older than she was, though she did not know by how many years.

It is widely believed that female 'circumcision' in Kapchorwa is associated with witchcraft and evil spirits. Cherotich, a one-time circumciser and mentor, revealed a great deal of information to me about all the myths and stories surrounding female 'circumcision'.

"In our day," she began, "a long time ago, the elders glorified the practice of 'circumcision'. By the time I reached the age of sixteen, I already had the courage to go for it. Together with my age-mates, we encouraged each other and prepared for it.

"Our parents paid the 'circumcision' fee, and for about four months, beginning in August, we trained each other in dancing styles specifically designed for the ritual. We danced on the rocky paths as we waited for the month of December, when the 'circumcision' date would be communicated to us.

"Our parents had brewed beer, and when the day came, there was a lot of drinking and celebrating. We danced all night with the mentors as the circumcisers sharpened their knives. At dawn the following day, we were taken to a river to clean our genitals in preparation for the cutting. When we were ready, we sang songs glorifying our culture as we walked to the 'circumcision' grounds. When we reached the place, the circumcisers were already waiting for us under a shelter constructed specifically for the occasion.

"The 'circumcision' takes place at dawn because the circumcisers need enough light to clearly see where to cut. At the grounds, a ram was slaughtered, and all the first-born daughters were smeared with chyme. After that ritual was completed, we were ordered to lie down on a mat. One girl at a time, the surgeon cut out the labia and clitoris in a matter of seconds. In this way, we were initiated into womanhood and were to become role models as adults in our community.

"After being circumcised, I felt that I had become a heroine and deserved the respect that all circumcised women in the community received. Shortly after 'circumcision', my parents found me a man to marry, and before a year elapsed, we were married and had started living as husband and wife. We bore children, and I must confess that the gods showered their favour upon me because, unlike other women, I did not experience any complications while giving birth. Even during sexual intercourse with my husband, I did not feel any pain, and I lived a normal life. The only pain I felt was immediately after I was cut, and it disappeared after a few days.

"I had a happy family of two sons and a loving husband who, I must confess, was much older than I was. Unfortunately, my husband and children have all passed away, and now I am all alone. Ever since I lost my husband, in 1993, I have felt so lonely, completely deserted because I have no one to look after me in my old age.

"Before I became a circumciser, I was attacked by spirits. As a result I went mad. I wandered and ran around without cause or direction. It all started in the year 1957, when I began having weird dreams, and then I menstruated for the whole year without stopping. Because the bleeding persisted, my people decided to visit a diviner, who revealed to them that the spirits of my grandparents had returned and had chosen me to engage in the 'circumcision' of the Sabiny girls. You know, these days witchdoctors are not truthful like they used to be. In those days, it was easy to discern truth from falsehood.

"I come from a line of circumcisers. I must have inherited the disposition from my father's lineage because my father's aunt was a circumciser. Unfortunately, this family tradition did not stop with me. The spirits disturbed my younger sister Amina as well, because they also wanted her to become a circumciser. They would take her to the river, to the forest, and to caves, and we would look for her and eventually find her in those hidden places.

"I started circumcising in 1957 and continued until 1960, when I retired. It is interesting how I was inaugurated into the world of 'circumcision'. I was given 'circumcision' tools and other cultural items. The elders organised a ceremony and performed cultural rituals linking me to the gods as I received the tools. They prepared local beer and they spat it on my face and all over my body. During such rituals, the drink is either sprinkled on you from a broom that has been dipped in a beer pot, or it is spat all over your body, as they did in my case. As the beer was falling on me, the elders handed over the tools, including the knife and a whetstone for sharpening it. You see, you do not sharpen the 'circumcision' knife on just any stone. Everything is special.

"During the years I was a circumciser, I cut many girls. It is hard for me to calculate the number, but my estimate is at least twenty girls per day each December in even-numbered years. Sometimes a few families were not ready and didn't have the means to organise the feasts. Some parents could not afford to buy meat and beer for the people, and that was an obstacle. It meant that some girls dropped out and had to wait for another season."

"That means that it is economically a strain on some families, doesn't it?" I interrupted her.

"Yes, of course," Saina responded. "It is expensive, but each family tries as much as possible to have their daughters circumcised because it is believed that 'circumcision' is a prerequisite for marriage, and here women are largely economically dependent on men.

"In addition, a girl who is not circumcised is generally considered a coward and a weakling and therefore not worth marrying. A girl who does not have her clitoris removed is considered a great challenge in terms of sexual appetite and, ultimately, is fatal to a man. I can't explain some of these things to you, but for personal reasons, these days I no longer circumcise girls. As much as it is being fought today, however, I want you to know that 'circumcision' is still going on secretly. Girls sneak into the deep forests of Kapchorwa to be cut there.

"When I was still circumcising, I never sterilised my knife or changed knives during the rituals, but at that time, AIDS was still unknown to most of us. Once it started spreading, all circumcisers were advised and cautioned against using the same knife to cut all the girls. The health authorities advised them to at least sterilise their knives in hot water if they could not afford to use different knives.

"As a circumciser, I enjoyed a number of benefits. Each 'circumcision' candidate would pay me a fee and also bring me chickens and good food. These kept me very healthy and gave me more energy to cut and keep the culture alive and strong. The candidates benefited too. In the course of visiting their kin to announce their upcoming 'circumcision', they would be given gifts of chickens, goats, and sometimes cows.

"During 'circumcision', the girls are made to lie down with their legs wide open. Unlike men, who are supposed to face up when they are being circumcised, the girls are instructed to turn their heads to the right as the surgeon prepares to cut. The surgeon then picks up some coarsely ground millet flour and sprinkles it on the labia and clitoris to stop the area from being slippery. This helps to make it easy to hold and cut the body parts.

"If a girl screams in pain during the cutting, she is considered to be a very weak woman. Such weaklings are left for married men who are looking for second wives, or they are given to disabled or mentally impaired men in the community who have failed to marry. Able-bodied men are not permitted to marry such cowardly women because they are a big embarrassment and a disgrace to society.

"I used to spend the whole night sharpening my knife with the other circumcisers. Since the other circumcisers would drink and smoke during the night, they had an added advantage because they kept themselves busy. My Muslim religion does not permit me to do those things. Anyway, most of the circumcisers are not attached to their religions because they are possessed by spirits that instruct them on cultural issues," Saina said.

As I tried to work out the contradiction between what is expected of her as a Muslim and what is bequeathed to her by the spirits, she went on to say, "But currently people are refusing to listen to the spirits because they are more engrossed in religion.

"While sharpening our knives, we didn't talk much. We would occasionally talk to the mentors, since they were our apprentices. They helped us to carry our tools and other material.

"I was committed to my work as a circumciser, which made me fast and popular. Within a short time I could go through twenty candidates, and then I would quickly proceed to another village to circumcise even more girls, during the same early morning. The speed went hand in hand with the craft. I should also add that no candidate of mine ever got any complications after being cut because I was pretty skilled at my job. This shows how committed I was to it.

"Sometimes the circumcisers failed to cut out the labia completely, and then they would have to go back and do the cutting again. The mentors closely monitored the girls until they completely healed. They also imparted to them all the cultural values and the post-'circumcision' secrets. The mentor ensured that the required amount of cutting had been done. If she saw that some parts were not cut properly, then she would call back the circumciser to trim the flesh down to the required level. But in most cases, if the circumciser was out of reach, the mentor would complete the job. At that stage, the pain was worse than the pain at the first instance."

When I asked Saina what happened to the body parts that they cut, she laughed lightly and said, "It is the duty of the mentor to collect all the parts of the participants after they have been circumcised. It is a cultural norm that these girls (now women) are not allowed to bathe for three days after being cut. When the three days have passed, the body parts are then thrown away or buried in an undisclosed place. That is our secret.

"Now I will tell you a bit about the 'circumcision' of twins. There are some rituals that have to be carried out before twins are circumcised. These are very different and more complicated than for ordinary children. When a twin has lost the mother or father or the child that followed her or him, the elders, along with the mentors and circumcisers, go to the grave of the deceased and remove the deceased's bones. The bones are then placed in a basket and carried in a procession of elders, with the twin and all other candidates awaiting 'circumcision'. The whole procession moves along dancing and singing traditional songs.

"But these days it is different. In case any of the above died, the elders would just go to the place where they hid the mother of the twins after childbirth, as is the tradition. In Sabiny culture, when a woman produces twins, she is hidden in a house for some time before she is brought out and unveiled to society. That house is the place where the twins will be taken in preparation for 'circumcision'. Soil is dug out of this house, a goat is killed, the blood is mixed with the soil, and then the mixture is smeared on the twins, after which they will be ready for 'circumcision'.

"In Sabiny culture, immediately after twins are born, a hole is dug and a particular green tree is planted in it. Leaves from this tree, called takamuda, are then mixed with the intestines of a sheep that has been slaughtered for the ritual. The mixture is then used to smear the parents of the twins, and the rest of the carcass is buried. The mother of the twins is then hidden in the house for some time, and after subsequent rituals have been performed, she is free to mingle with other people.

"After all the rituals have been performed, the green tree is watered and well-tended. The house is also held sacred. When the twins come of age, soil is dug from around the base of the tree and used to smear the heads of the twins, and then they are taken to a cave. When they return from the cave, they are taken back to the house where the tree was planted. That tree is then uprooted, and a cowhide is laid down, with the trunk of the tree on top. The twins then stand on the hide. This is believed to prevent them from bleeding and going into shock when they are circumcised.

"The rules and standards for circumcising twins are so strict that a twin cannot get circumcised if her mother has not been cut. If she is a non-Sabiny woman married to a Sabiny man, there is absolutely no problem, but if an uncircumcised Sabiny woman produced the twins, she must be circumcised first, before recognising her as a mother of twins. There is no way the mother can dodge 'circumcision' after producing twins because shortly after their birth, the twins and their mother are hidden in the house, and before they are brought out, the mother must be circumcised.

"However, sometimes a mother of twins dies after giving birth. If she was not circumcised, her body cannot be passed through the main entrance of the house. The back of the house is broken into, and her body is passed out through the backyard. This is to show any women who think of avoiding the practice that even in death they will be regarded as social outcasts and carried to their graves in humiliation.

"In Sabiny culture, it is taboo to fail to circumcise both twins, but there are cases where an exception can be made. For instance, if one of them is too sickly and it is well known that she might not survive the pain of 'circumcision', she will be exempted, but on condition that she stands by the side of the twin who is being cut. There is really no way a twin can be circumcised if her sister is not standing beside her, unless she is dead. In that case, her grave will be dug up and her bones scooped out and brought to the 'circumcision' grounds.

"After 'circumcision', twins are treated the same as the other girls. The elders believe that to quickly heal, the girls have to urinate on their wound. In my time, there was no treatment after 'circumcision' except urine. The girls were forced to urinate frequently, crossing their legs and holding them together tightly. They did this for two weeks, and by the third week they would have healed. Any girl found to be holding in her urine would be flogged.

"Traditionally, the girls are not allowed to use water for bathing. They are only allowed to use sap squeezed out of banana stems into a calabash or pot. And the first bath they are allowed will be three days after they are cut.

"After 1960, I surrendered my 'circumcision' duties to my younger sister, Amina, but I volunteered to help her in mentoring the girls. As a mentor, one of my duties was to administer traditional herbs to the girls during 'circumcision'. The rationale was to change the childish attitude of the girl and give her a sense of maturity so that she would become a strong and respectable woman in society. On the eve of 'circumcision', the girls are made to dance as they visit their kin and friends. Then they are given food and drinks, and after that they are taken to a room where cultural secrets are revealed to them, with a strong caution not to tell any of the secrets to anyone. They are also given a small portion of a certain herb to strengthen them during the actual cutting. The night before the candidates are cut, they go through certain cultural processes, and the pain they encounter then is actually equal to that of the cutting itself.

"Another role I assumed as a mentor was to take the girls through the oath of secrecy, as to the cultural lore of the tribe. As Sabiny, we treasure certain cultural secrets, and the girls know that it is taboo to reveal these to any person, including their very own blood relations, especially those who have not gone through the initiation process. If you reveal those secrets, you will be cursed, and because of the restrictions surrounding such revelations, I am not in a position to reveal them to you even if you threaten me with a knife or a gun. I would rather die than betray my people. Any one who tells the secrets will either go mad or be struck dead."

Saina looked at me with a serious expression as she told me this, and I was forced to ask her whether she had ever witnessed anyone running mad or dying as a result of revealing the Sabiny secrets.

"I must confess that I actually do not know anyone in my village who has run mad or died, but I have heard so many stories of women in other places who have had this happen because they violated the oath of secrecy. Cultural beliefs should not be taken lightly," she said, as if sounding a warning. "I have been asked before whether as a circumciser I was involved in the cursing, since I was a kind of cultural goddess, but that is a question that I cannot answer. Even if I had been involved, I would not tell you anything concerning witchcraft because it is against the rules of my culture. We keep all our secrets."

As Saina spoke, I began to feel anxious about my mission of finding out the secrets that are the driving force behind the knife. I asked her to comment on the marks I see on her arm, but she refused. "That too is taboo to reveal," she said.

Before the interview, I had been told that, according to Sabiny culture, after a circumcised woman has healed, she is taken to the forest, where she fights with a leopard that scratches her arm and makes the four marks. It is also believed that the women who have short scratches are stronger than the women with long scratches because they are thought to have overpowered the leopard before it made long scratches on them. Indeed, most Sabiny women have scratches of different lengths. Of course, others say that it is the mentors and circumcisers themselves who scratch the timid girls in the dark bush. But I wanted Saina to tell me the truth about it.

Cultures normally have their own specific music and forms of drama, and it is evident that the Sabiny are passionate about their culture and express it through song. During the preparation for initiation, all the candidates are taught traditional songs and dances that they must learn before they can be initiated into adulthood. The songs sound vulgar, and the dances are quite seductive. One of the songs Saina gave me is a factual song that explains the pain of the practice and the transformative effect it has on the candidate. It transforms you from a child into an adult, and in the process you are recognised in the community as somebody of high standing.

If you have accepted, you accept until the very end.
If you can't manage, please go away because it is a painful experience.
So you have to endure.
Killing you by an arrow is even better and less painful than 'circumcision'.
So if you feel you prefer an arrow and want to remain a girl please go away.
You still have a long clitoris.
You are just a girl.
If you get a short a one, you will become a real Sabiny woman.

Saina said she no longer wants to associate herself with 'circumcision'. "I would not wish to become a circumciser again because government has now criminalised the practice, and I fear being hunted by the long arm of the law. Besides, my successor, Amina, has also given up the practice, so why would I go back to it? On the other hand, I am undecided on the issue of 'circumcision' itself. Those people trying to stop the practice should see to it that they provide for the women circumcisers they are stopping from continuing, because that is how they earn their living. If I do not get any assistance, then I am ready to go back to circumcising even if they have criminalised it. Currently, some people have become thieves owing to their poverty, and this year I am willing to circumcise secretly just to earn a little money.

"I used to sell fruits and vegetables, but now I have become very sick and weak and cannot work. Old age is a limitation to me, and the money that REACH gives me is too little to sustain me. I do not repent at all for earning my living from 'circumcision', and I can only pretend to adjust to modern ways of thinking about it. How about those people who slaughter animals, do they feel sorry for killing the animals or do they rejoice that they are going to eat meat? If the government had not made it a criminal offence, I would continue encouraging the 'circumcision' of girls."

After this very long and interesting conversation, I understood that the Sabiny culture is still deeply entrenched, and that trying to eradicate it is like chasing a mirage in the desert. Some of the Sabiny elders have converted themselves from proponents to opponents of female genital cutting. They have attracted the attention of international health and population experts through finding their own way to deal with a practice that is widely condemned by women's groups.

We can only hope and pray that one day all the mist and smoke will be cleared from everyone's eyes and they will see clearly, understanding that the girl child is as important as the male child and that some cultural practices, especially female genital mutilation, cause more harm than good. The sun will surely shine very brightly on the day that all the 'circumcision' knives and razors are destroyed and peace is bestowed on the soul of the girl child in Kapchorwa. Hope, don't die!

Hilda Twongyeirwe

Run (For my sisters)

Run
my daughter run
run
to that far away land
run
where man's heart has no holes
run
before it's too late
run
my daughter
run
away from the raucous noise of the blades
run
where flowers are let to blossom
run
my daughter run
run
where full rings adorn fingers
run
without looking back
run
and rally behind you those lingering on the road
run
run
my daughter run
run
and return when wholeness is on reign.
Run …

Beatrice Lamwaka

The Missing Letter in the Alphabet

I am not supposed to be sitting on an empty bed weeping over a piece of paper on my wedding night. My relatives and Michael's are still at the hotel partying the night away. I can hear people talking in Kupsabiny and Acholi. My mother is enjoying the lavishness of her daughter's wedding. The décor by Archu was just as I had wanted it to be, green and white, matching my wedding gown. The taste of bruschetta and lasagne is still fresh in my mouth. Two glasses of Champagne remain on the table. African daffodils, a gift from the Sheraton Hotel, spread their pungent fragrance. Our wedding planner promised to deliver her best, and she didn't disappoint. Everything was as we had wanted. I am happy that my wedding was as I dreamt it would be. I worried about my gown, the food, the dancers, and the musicians -- but never did a problem with Michael cross my mind.

I almost wanted to believe my friend. "Chesha, my dear, don't get married to that Acholiman," she often said. I never listened. Of course, she knew I would not listen. I never listen to her anyway. I can't imagine that my marriage to Michael might end on our wedding night. For some reason, a life without Michael doesn't seem real to me. Whenever I think of my future, Michael is there with me.

I am sitting in my honeymoon suite, but without Michael snuggling me or doing what married people do - something that I had been looking forward to. I had visualised something memorable that I would write about and read to the two of us many years to come. Then we would all recall how nice it had been. I never thought that my wedding night would become something like this.

I can still feel Michael's fingers sliding over my thighs. His warm lips were as I had imagined this scene so many times. But when things start to happen differently, I am too shocked to know what to do.

"Baby," I keep calling him, as my aunt had taught me to do. He does not respond. He just stares into space. He is looking at something beyond my eyes.

He touches me, we touch each other. Then he stops. We stop.

"Michael," I say.

"Yes?" he responds. His voice is husky. It traps me.

"We talked about this," I say to him. My voice is very faint. I can hardly hear myself.

We had chatted on Facebook about my condition, but maybe he did not understand.

"You didn't tell me it was like this," he says as he slowly removes his fingers from between my legs.

"It's not my fault, you know," I tell him.

"I know. I know... But I can't ... we just can't ... I am not saying it is your fault," he says. I watch him reach for his clothes. The trousers. His shirt. His necktie. Stony silence sits between us. I tell myself I will not cry.

"Let's talk. Please," I beg him. But he is not listening. He is not looking at me. "Please," I say again.

"No. Not now," he says as he walks out of the room. I call after him, but my voice remains in the room. He shuts the door behind him.

That is how I end up coiled on this bed, writing on this paper.

For me, the word "'circumcision'" means that my husband will stay with me and trust me. It does not mean that he will leave me in this bed alone, wrapped up in a new longing for him. I know I did not do anything wrong. All I did was what every girl in my community does. I was proud because the women sang me songs of praise. I was the bravest of all the girls. I was proud of my new status. My clitoris, the source of all evil, was dead and buried somewhere.

When I first learnt that at some point I would be circumcised, I was eleven years old. I was told 'circumcision' would make me a whole woman and keep me away from danger. My friends and I said the word "'circumcision'," but we didn't understand what it was. We only knew it was something that we had to undergo to be whole women. Something my friends and I talked about as we walked home from school. 'circumcision'. It was a familiar word. What was not clear was when our turn would come. It never occurred to me that when the day arrived, I would feel tingling in my panties or that I would have a near-death experience. My mother always brushed off my questions when 'circumcision' came up in our conversation, as if it were something minor that every woman experienced. So every time I saw an older woman, I knew that she had been circumcised. For me, that something was missing, and it was already buried somewhere. The letter "C" was missing in the alphabet of my womanhood. I am an incomplete alphabet whose husband has deserted. I am a dismantled alphabet puzzle whose missing parts cannot be found.

It is amazing how the husband quickly slides off the paper. Before we got married, when my friends teased me that Michael was my husband, I quickly corrected them. He is my boyfriend, I said with a smile. And now I am calling him my husband, but he is nowhere to be seen.

I want to shout out, "I am whole!" but I wonder who cares. My parents probably thought Michael was aware because they thought that Michael and I had already had sex so he knew I was circumcised. And who cares that only my clitoris is missing? I am whole. I am a woman. I am Michael's wife. I am me, Chesha.

Do I sound drunk? Maybe I should have drunk a little of the white wine on my table at the reception. My shoes were uncomfortable, and I didn't want to deal with the effect of the wine as well as the shoes. I didn't know that there would be a lot more I would have to deal with. I wish I could push back the time.

'Circumcision', the word is familiar. I remember the ordeal clearly. But it is the pain that will never stop. My wound healed fast, but the pain remained. I can still feel it. I dream about it, and it is so real. I don't know why my clitoris was cut, but I know that I will have to deal with the pain of Michael walking away from me on our wedding night.

I remember the day Michael and I met for the first time. A month after he sent me a friend request on Facebook. How much he was attracted to me. Nobody else had told me how the weight I was trying to fight off was sexy, or that my chunky lips were good for kissing. I was quickly in love with him. I couldn't stop thinking about him. When we set a date for our wedding one year later, I couldn't believe that it would actually happen. Everything with Michael was surreal. He attended Christian Ministries Church and was born again. We agreed that the best gift we would give each other on our wedding night was sex, and so we promised we would wait. I also wanted to wait because sex was not something on my mind. Maybe because my alphabet was incomplete. I knew that among the Acholi people the clitoris was never a problem, and it was left to grow as long as it did. People even said that in some cultures they pull and elongate their labia to build more poles to support the clitoris, more room for sensation.

During one of our late night chats, Michael said he was longing to touch me. That night he was really chatty. I could feel the waves in his words. He asked me whether I had pulled my genitals, and I told him that pulling was unheard of in our clan. He laughed and said he had heard about pulling from his friends and had hoped that I knew about it. I did not laugh with him as I usually did. He asked me what the pulling entailed, and I told him I did not know. Then I said that I did not even have a clitoris. He laughed again, louder this time, and said that I should permit him to check. I reminded him of our promise to wait for the wedding night, and I said I was serious. He continued laughing and said that he would not ask again.

Now I know that the words never got home. They may have lingered on Facebook chat and just waited to reach him today. On our wedding day. Today of all days. He has failed to be the Casanova that he always wanted to be.

I don't know how long I have been writing. I feel as if I am in a trance. I hear footsteps in the corridor. It sounds as if the person is wearing shoes that are too tight. They are squeezing her feet. The footsteps are not even. Maybe this is another tired woman or man. Maybe a man. Maybe Michael. I can hear the beating of my heart. If it is Michael, I will stop writing. I will hold him and never let him go. I remember I did not lock the door after he left. But I can't go to the door. I wait to hear him pass. I pray it's not a serial killer that checks open doors and strangles women. I hear my heart pounding loudly. I hold my breath and wait. Wait for my end. Wait for the footsteps to disappear. Wait for Michael.

The door opens. I scream in fright. But it is Michael. It's my husband.

"Honey, I am sorry." he says.

Tears flow down my cheeks. Michael holds me. My husband holds me. I drop the pen.

Salome Akwi

Veto the Cut

Today I become a woman
Or else I shall be shunned
In silence I sit around silhouetted young female figures,
Stunned and awaiting their turn

Here, listening to the joyous sound of ululation
Every time a candidate is unveiled
My soul aches with agitation
As culture is getting my future sealed

No! I must abscond
I will not succumb
To the cold sharp gleaming razor blade
Mercilessly ripping through my sensitive, tender being

Yes, flee I must;
For the sake of my generation
For being a factual beautiful woman
Not even the curses of my forefathers will stop me
I veto 'the cut'

Hon. Dora C. Kanabahita Byamukama

Postscript

Female Genital Mutilation (FGM) refers to "all procedures involving partial or total removal of the external female genitalia or other injury to the female organs for non-medical reasons" (World Health Organization). FGM traumatises girls and women in many ways, interfering with the natural functioning of the body and causing several immediate and long term consequences. For example, babies born to women who have undergone FGM suffer a higher rate of neonatal death than those of intact mothers.

Various social and religious reasons are advanced to justify continuing to cut, most premised on deep-rooted inequality between the sexes. An extreme form of gender discrimination, FGM violates human rights including the right to life when the procedure proves lethal; the right to be free from torture and cruel, inhuman or degrading treatment; and the right to health, security and physical integrity of the person.

In Uganda, work to eliminate FGM spans a period of over twenty years mainly focused on the Sabiny; recently it has expanded to cover areas of Busoga region, the Karamoja region, and areas populated by Nubians and Somali. Elimination of FGM can only be achieved by sensitizing practicing communities to abandon it.

One method deployed to stop FGM is enactment of a law that prohibits it. Uganda's Constitution implicitly forbids it; the Penal Code Act criminalizes it as grievous harm punishable by seven years imprisonment. In spite of these legal provisions, however, FGM is still practiced in Uganda. To date no law enforcement officer has used the Penal Code Act to arrest perpetrators of FGM who have hidden and shrouded their activities under the guise of culture and religion. The right to culture and religion is not absolute and cannot be upheld when it breaches other human rights such as the right to freedom from torture, cruel or inhuman and degrading treatment – which rights are absolute.

The law is an effective social engineering instrument; it is even more effective when it is specific and has legitimacy once the community appreciates the vices of FGM and is willing to abandon the custom. Laws that prohibit FGM, therefore, must be complemented by culturally sensitive education and public awareness-raising. For example, introduction of a Culture Day among the Sabiny and more recently among the Pokot is one good example that can be emulated elsewhere. The Culture Day is used in these communities to promote positive traditions and to create awareness about negative cultural practices. Where FGM is premised on religion, religious leader should clearly explain that FGM is not required.

National and international organizations have played a key role in advocating against FGM and generating data that confirm its harm. At the national level, the Uganda Constitution and Penal Code Act are instrumental as is passage of a specific law against FGM in 2009. At the Africa regional level, the protocol to the African Charter on Human and People's Rights on the Rights of Women in Africa specifically calls for elimination of FGM.

Law and Advocacy for Women in Uganda (LAW-Uganda), in partnership with Reproductive, Educative and Community Health Programme (REACH), United Nations Population Fund (UNFPA), Vital Voices, Ministry of Gender, Labour and Social Development, United Nations Children's Fund (UNICEF), Uganda Women's Parliamentary Association (UWOPA), Food Security, Population FORUM and SEA have used various innovative methods against FGM. FEMRITE joins the fight with yet another tool of personal testimonies.

I wish to commend FEMRITE –Uganda Women Writers Association for breaking the silence and recording voices of women that have been stifled for ages about the unhuman act. This protest is vital in the fight against FGM which received the highest political support when the President of the Republic of Uganda His Excellency Yoweri Kaguta Museveni declared the Government's opposition on July 1, 2009, in Amudat, Karamoja region. This noble and heroic action greatly catalysed action to eliminate FGM in Uganda.

The demise of the custom in Uganda and elsewhere is possible once the fight is led by leaders and members of communities where it has been maintained. There is need therefore for continued sensitization and efforts to establish mechanisms for prevention and rehabilitation of victims. A law without community support may not bear fruit.

This book captures the details, engages you in personal stories, and drives home the point that you must act now. Its voices that traverse boundaries make it a vital tool for use in sensitization campaigns at all levels in and outside Uganda.

Join in the action to Stop Female Genital Mutilation NOW.

Aluta Continua ...

Violet Barungi

Afterword

It is incredible that in Uganda today, indeed in the world there is still a protracted form of violence being committed against women in the name of tradition. This criminal act is in the nature of female genital mutilation (FGM), which violates women's human rights to enjoy their God-given gift of womanhood. These pages introduce a woman who could not have children as a result of undergoing 'circumcision'; another is permanently confined to a wheelchair after becoming paralysed due to long-term effects of the procedure. She is lucky because her two mates, circumcised at the same time, have since died after enduring ill health and excruciating pain for a long time. Other women cannot enjoy marital bliss because they have dysfunctional sexual relationships with their partners that bring them no enjoyment but instead untold physical and emotional pain. Some have been abandoned by their spouses because they cannot discharge their marital obligation to their husbands' satisfaction, never mind that being circumcised is prerequisite for a woman to find a husband. Circumcised women suffer more than their uncircumcised counterparts, and more often than not, have to undergo a Caesarean while birthing their offspring. These women represent millions of others in the world, especially in Africa where the practice is most prevalent.

FGM -- gender-based violence against women -- is carried out in various parts of the world but is more concentrated in Africa. The practice violates their rights and the rights of the girl-child. As the testimonies in this collection show, FGM subjects women to many health hazards, including the spread of HIV/AIDS, incapacitation, fistula, and in some instances even death. It denies women and girl children self-determination, good health, liberty, security, dignity and the right to education. It also subjects them to torture.

Article 1 of the UN Convention on torture defines it as 'any act by which severe pain and suffering, whether physical or mental is intentionally inflicted on a person..." The Constitution of Uganda implicitly prohibits FGM under Article 24 which states that "no person shall be subjected to any form of torture or cruel, unhuman or degrading treatment ... Laws, cultures, customs and traditions which are against the dignity, welfare or interest of women ... or which undermine their status are prohibited by the Constitution. ..."

Despite the laws, FGM, more specifically in the regions of Kapchorwa and Pokota, is still a cherished, integral aspect of the culture. However, NGOs like REACH have been in Kapchorwa since 1996 trying to sensitize communities about the custom's serious health effects and advocating elimination. They have set up counselling centres for FGM victims and support for those who wish to rehabilitate their lives by going back to school. They also try to encourage women circumcisers to give up the business and find an alternative source of income.

The testimonies in this collection depict various experiences but they all revolve around the same axis: the inhumanity of FGM. Tradition shrouds the practice in mystery and superstition in order to make women more compliant and subservient to archaic and irrelevant societal norms that don't take their welfare into consideration.

However, the good news is that FGM is now a topic of public debate, with activists and right-thinking people advocating to stop it. Many countries in the world, including Ghana, Guinea, Djibouti, Burkina Faso, Central African Republic, Cote d'Ivoire, Tanzania, Togo, Senegal, Canada, USA, Sweden, Norway, Australia and the UK have outlawed FGM. Here in Uganda legislation against FGM was passed on December 10, 2009, and it is hoped that punitive measures will prove strong enough to act as deterrents. The president himself, on a visit to Karamoja, came out strongly to condemn the practice and support its prohibition.

FEMRITE hopes that after reading these perturbing testimonies by FGM victims, women and young girls in all parts of Uganda, Somalia, Ethiopia and the rest of the world where 'circumcision' is still imposed will take the necessary step to denounce the barbaric tradition and reclaim their rights, living normal lives and enjoying full womanhood as intended by their creator. This change of attitude will need wide and persuasive sensitization, facilitation by effective legislation, practical support, protection of FGM victims and encouragement of civil society.

We wish to extend our most sincere gratitude to Artaction for financial support that made this project possible. We are grateful to Iga Zinunura and Julius Ocwinyo who proofread the manuscript [of the original version, *Beyond the Dance*]. We are also very grateful to the story-tellers; it cannot have been easy for them to relive such painful experiences. Many thanks go to the scriptwriters, too, whose empathy and sensitivity to the sufferings of their fellow women make this collection compelling and informative reading.

Prose Contributors

Betty Kituyi is a published writer. Currently, she works with Café Scientific. She is also a peace activist and belongs to Uganda Peace Research Association and International Peace Research Association. She is passionate about women's and girl-child issues, and she co-ordinates two grass-root women's groups in her village. She also belongs to Bushunya environmental group where she helps in mobilising the community about environmental issues and sustainability. Betty Kituyi holds a master's degree in science, a Bachelor of Education degree, and a diploma in secondary education. She hails from Mbale, in eastern Uganda.

Bananuka Jocelyn Ekochu is a published writer whose first novel, Shockwaves Across the Ocean, was nominated for the International IMPAC DUBLIN Literary Award 2006. Jocelyn was born in Mbarara District, western Uganda. She attended Rutooma Integrated Primary School, Bweranyangyi Girls Senior Secondary School, and Makerere University Business School, where she earned a higher diploma in marketing and a Bachelor of Commerce degree. She holds a Postgraduate Diploma in Financial Management and a master's degree in management studies from Uganda Management Institute. Jocelyn is passionate about women's issues. She is a member of Women of Purpose, a faith-based association aimed at supporting the less-advantaged women and girls of Uganda.

Sharon Lamwaka is a freelance journalist who writes on gender and human rights issues. Sharon works with the African Centre for the Treatment of Torture Victims (ACTV) as a communications and advocacy officer. She holds a degree in journalism and a Master of Psychology degree. Sharon previously worked with Akina Mama Wa Africa, an international women's organisation whose headquarters are now in Uganda.

Lillian Tindyebwa was born in Rukungiri District in southern Uganda. She holds a Bachelor of Arts and a master's degree in literature. Her first novel, Recipe for Disaster, was published by Fountain Publishers and became an instant success when it was recommended by the Ministry of Education and Sports as a supplementary reader for all secondary schools in Uganda. She has also published a number of short stories and poems in different anthologies.

Ndagijimana Waltraud was born on July 9, 1949, in Neuss, Germany. She graduated from school in 1972 at Aachen, Germany. She now lives in Mutolere, Bufumbira, Kisoro District and teaches literature at St. Gertrude Girls' Secondary School Mutolere. Waltraud is a published author of short stories and poems in various anthologies. Her short story, "The Key," was dramatized and broadcast on BBC World Service in 1996.

Cathy Anite holds a Bachelor of Laws degree and is currently pursuing a diploma in legal practice. This is her maiden story, but she has also published poems in anthologies.

Maryam Sheikh Abdi is a program officer for the Population Council's Reproductive Health program based in Nairobi, Kenya. Abdi works on a project that aims to accelerate the abandonment of female genital mutilation (FGM) in the Somali community of North Eastern Province of Kenya, where over 98 percent of girls are cut in the most severe form. Abdi previously worked for the UN High Commissioner for Refugees, the UN World Food Programme, and CARE. She holds a Master of Development Studies from the University of Nairobi and a Bachelor of Education from Moi University.

Hilda Twongyeirwe Rutagonya is passionate about women's issues and has initiated a number of writing projects aimed at making heard the voice of the marginalised woman. Her short stories, poems, and literary articles have appeared in journals and magazines. In 2008, she was awarded a certificate of recognition for her outstanding contribution to children's literature for her book, Fina the Dancer. She has also published other children's books in Rukiga Runyankore, courtesy of Longhorn Publishers. Hilda serves on the Board of Directors of the National Book Trust, the Arterial Network Uganda Chapter's Executive Committee, and is a member of the Banyakigezi International Community, Uganda Chapter. She holds an M.A. in Public Administration and Management, a degree in social sciences, and a diploma in education. She hails from Kacerere, in Kabale District, western Uganda. Currently she is the coordinator of FEMRITE.

Beatrice Lamwaka from Alokolum, Gulu, Uganda, is a writer whose short story "Butterfly Dreams" was shortlisted for the 2011 Caine Prize. An executive board member of FEMRITE since 1998, she is also plays a leadership role as founder and director of the Arts Therapy Foundation and served as general secretary of Uganda's section of PEN. See https://en.wikipedia.org/wiki/Beatrice_Lamwaka

Rebecca Salonen, an editor at the University of Bridgeport, founded Godparents Association, a registered tax-exempt charity, in 1998 to stop FGM through education. Sponsors support girls who want to escape being cut; Godparents Assocation pays their school fees. In addition, as the website states, "Donations of unrestricted funds less than the amount needed to sponsor a girl are used to hold tutoring or motivational workshops or are pooled to pay fees for secondary-school graduates attending universities." Salonen has been publishing a Newsletter monthly since 1998, available through the website. See http://www.godparents.net

Hon. Dora C. Kanabahita Byamukama is a polician, Member of the East African Legislative Assembly and Director, Law and Advocacy for Women in Uganda.

Poets include

Plucking a Rose Bud	Dorah Musiimire
Tonight	Jemeo Nanyonjo
I am already a woman!	Grace Atuhaire
Sacrilege	Lindah Niwenyesiga
All for Tradition	Linda Lilian
The Ungodly Scalpel	Tezira Jamwa
The Unwilling Sacrificial Lamb	Linda Lillian
Walking on these Heavy Hills	Alal Sophie Brenda
I say no more!	Jennifer A. Okech
Pruning	Barbara Oketta
Her Last Word	Margaret Ntakalimaze
The Cut	Maryam Sheikh Abdi
Vultures of Culture	Sophie Bamwoyeraki
My Sister learns her ABC	Beverly Nambozo Nsengiyunva
My Mother's wish	Brenda Lubwama
In Kapchorwa	Alal Sopphie Brenda
A little time	Allen Atutambira
SAY 'NO"	
(Translated from Amharic)	Wudalat Gedamu (Ethiopia)
Threshold	Hilda Twongyeirwe
Veto the Cut	Salome Akwi

163

Each UnCUT/VOICES Press book supports a specific project against FGM. Sales of Taboo contribute to the **Clitoris Restoration Fund** that sponsors operations by Dr. Pierre Foldes at the Institut en Santé Génésique in St. Germain-en-Laye outside Paris, France.

In the United States, your donation is tax deductible. Send a check in any amount made out to **Healthy Tomorrow** with a clear notation that you are contributing to the Clitoris Restoration Fund.
The address: Healthy Tomorrow, 14 William St., Somerville, MA 02144 USA.

You can also make a tax-deductible contribution in Germany by bank transfer to FORWARD –Germany with the clear notation **Clitoris Restoration Fund and your email or snail-mail address.** (For tax deduction in other European nations, please ask your income tax authority if they accept a German Spendenquittung/ receipt.)
Transfer to
FORWARD – Germany e.V.
Frankfurter Sparkasse
BLZ 500 502 01
Account # 200029398
IBAN: DE20 5005 0201 0200 0293 98
BIC SWIFT: HELADEF1822

Jeanie Kortum

Afterthoughts

On the mountaintop in Uganda a women begins to tell the story of her life. Just one single voice but the story floats towards us across the continents, her words lyrical and beautiful. "To whee, to whee," she adds the sound of an owl and now here come bells, whistles and chatter; a party is happening in her village. Her story fills our hungry ears. Because she is a natural storyteller we are rocked in the sway of her words, made childlike again, lullaby softened. ... But wait, something is happening. A feeling of malevolence has entered her words, blood and secrets buried in the innocent cadence. She adds the sound of screams, tears; the narrator pulls herself through the mud and then when the mutilation finally happens and her vagina is cut, some of the violation and shock enters our bodies as well, listening now unbearable for we know 1 million women's stories exist inside this one.

"The woman in me died at the hands of the circumciser," she states. "I closed my mind to who I was and what was happening."

Her words enter us deeply. We can almost see her— hurt, bewildered and scared, she is only a little girl. She claws her hair, her eyes dart to the left, to the right, her cheeks wear the sheen of tears. "Circumcision is not something a woman chooses to do," she tells us. "It is what she has to do." The lurid act performed on her arrives ringing to our own bodies, enters the province of our own sexuality and sisterhood. Listening to her heartfelt eloquence, riding the wings of good storytelling, far away on another continent, we lick the salt of her tears from our cheeks.

www.ingramcontent.com/pod-product-compliance
Lightning Source LLC
Chambersburg PA
CBHW020654260626
47157CB00008B/3027